Gunshots and Gelato

By Richard Lucchesi

Gunshots and Gelato
Copyright © 2026 by Richard Lucchesi

For privacy reasons, some names, locations and dates may have been changed.

This publication is designed to provide accurate information based upon the author's experiences. It is sold with the understanding that neither the author nor the publisher is engaged in rendering legal advice or professional services. They make no warranties with respect to the accuracy or completeness of the contents of this book. The advice and experiences herein may not be suitable for your situation. You should consult a professional when appropriate.

Book Cover by Stephanie Ishler.

For Silvia Fossati

Table of Contents

"For anyone whose life ever exploded into madness the moment they said, "I'm just going to Italy for a fresh start."

— Unknown

Chapter 1 – The Road to Montaione

Cassidy Moore would have loved to say that after surviving Siena's tunnels, a kidnapping, a conspiracy involving weaponized honey, and a black truffle etched with the word *REVELARE*, she finally felt calm.

But no.

Life, apparently, didn't hand out calm in Tuscany.

Instead, she found herself standing in a half-ruined courtyard behind a bakery in Siena, surrounded by the people who were now, for better or worse, the only ones she'd trust with her life — Lorenzo, Giacomo, Adriano, Nonna Vivi, and Silvia — all of them facing off against a man in a cheap suit whose entire personality screamed: *I do contract work for villains and take no pride in it.*

The man adjusted his tie — a thin, shiny, too-short atrocity that looked like it cost seven euros and a prayer — and said,

"You can hand over the ledger quietly, or I can forcibly remove it from your—"

"Oh my God," Cassidy blurted. "That tie is a crime scene."

Adriano muttered, "Cassidy…"

"No, really," she whispered. "He looks like an accountant for evil clowns."

Silvia snorted, unable to hold it back. The man glared.

Cassidy really should have backed up and explained herself.

Because right at that moment, her life looked like a spaghetti bowl of bad decisions — beautiful, confusing, saucy — and somehow all roads were now leading to Montaione.

Her Life Fell Apart and Got Better and Then Fell Apart Again

Cassidy came to Italy for a fresh start. Instead, she got:

- a guesthouse that wasn't actually hers,
- a maddeningly cryptic — and unfairly hot — Italian named Adriano,

1

- a dead woman whose recipes hid a secret code,
- syrupy conspiracies spanning oils, vinegars, and honey,
- a son (Lorenzo… not hers, Giulia's) with secrets of his own,
- hills full of truffles,
- a kidnapped Nonna,
- and a cryptic truffle inscribed with the word REVELARE, basically saying: *Hey Cassidy, hope you're well — please unravel international food crime.*
- And finally: discovering her own mother was not who she thought she was, and that her entire life now somehow felt like a lie.

Fine. Sure. Why not?

But now, the group had Nonna Vivi back, rescued from a hidden Siena tunnel like some kind of culinary oracle. They had the ledger — Cassidy's mother's ledger — the key to an antidote for a slow-acting poison hidden in the honey supply.

And all that stood between them and synthesizing the antidote was one rare ingredient: *Asphodel.*

A wild flower that grew near Montaione.

And according to Lorenzo?

"You don't find asphodel," he had told them. "Asphodel finds you."

Terrifying.

Back to the Cheap Suit Villain

"You have something that belongs to my employer," the man sneered.

"Yes," Nonna Vivi replied in her basil-and-brimstone voice. "My foot."

Everyone paused — including the villain.

"Scusi?" he said.

She lifted her cane. "Would you like it?"

Giacomo stepped forward and cracked his knuckles. "She means she will hit you."

"I got that," the cheap-suit man said.

Lorenzo, ever polite, smiled with hospitality that barely veiled a threat.

"Listen, my friend. You should leave before this becomes… what is the phrase Cassidy uses?"

Cassidy perked up. "A dumpster fire covered in bees?"

"Yes." Lorenzo nodded. "That."

The man put a hand inside his jacket in a very classic villain move.

Adriano stepped between him and the group. "Be careful."

The man hesitated. His eyes flicked to Adriano's shoulders, then to Giacomo's arms, then to Nina — who had silently appeared behind him like a furry assassin.

"Is… is that dog staring at me?" he croaked.

"Yes," Silvia said sweetly. "And she bites people with bad fashion sense."

"I do not—"

Nina growled.

The man ran.

"Coward!" Nonna Vivi shouted after him. "Your tie is cheap and your tailor lies to you!"

Silence fell over the courtyard.

Lorenzo dusted off his hands. "Okay. Now that that is settled… we must get to Montaione before sunset."

The Plan — Or What Passed For One

They circled up — their squad of misfits, chefs, one American with shaky life choices, and a Nonna with the spiritual energy of a grenade.

"We need the asphodel flower," Adriano said. "Without it, we cannot finish the antidote."

3

"The poison will continue spreading," Silvia added. "Every jar, every bottle, every shipment—"

"It will not reach that point," Nonna Vivi said firmly. "We stop it now."

Cassidy?

Not emotionally ready for a global honey disaster.

But sure, let's go.

"How far is Montaione from Siena?" she asked.

"About an hour and a half," Lorenzo replied. "More if we take scenic backroads."

He paused.

"With us... we will take scenic backroads."

"I have a vineyard contact there," he continued. "A friend. Old friend. Supplier of ingredients for my classes. He owes me favors."

"He also has a big property," Silvia chimed in. "A good place to hide. To work."

"And rest," Adriano added, glancing at Nonna Vivi.

Giacomo straightened. "Speaking of which — Nonna Vivi must not come. I will bring her to my mother's aunt's cousin's house."

Cassidy blinked. "Is... that a real person?"

"Yes," Giacomo said simply. "And she is terrifying. No one will touch Nonna Vivi there."

"What is her name?" Cassidy asked.

"Brunella."

The name alone made Cassidy straighten her posture.

"She will be safe," Giacomo said. "But she cannot take another chase."

Nonna Vivi rolled her eyes dramatically. "I can still sprint."

"No," Adriano said gently. "You will rest. Let us finish this."

She huffed. "Fine. But if anyone gets stabbed, call me."

Silvia laughed. "We'll try."

Is There a Car Problem?

4

"So," Cassidy said, "six of us need to get to Montaione, but Italian cars are basically pocket-sized."

"Correct," Lorenzo said.

"And we don't have a car," Cassidy added.

"Also correct."

"We cannot take a stolen one," Adriano said.

Silvia sighed. "We *should not* take a stolen one."

"But we..." Giacomo raised a hand timidly. "We could borrow a Fiat Panda from my cousin?"

Adriano pinched the bridge of his nose. "Giacomo. The Panda fits maybe three people."

"It fits four if you believe."

"No."

"It fits five if you do not value skeletal integrity."

"NO."

Giacomo shrugged.

"So we need..." Cassidy prompted.

"Motorcycles," Lorenzo said simply.

Cassidy blinked. "We need what now?"

"Motorcycles," he repeated. "Three. One for me. One for Adriano. One for you."

"For me?" Cassidy echoed.

"Fine," Lorenzo amended. "Cassidy rides with Adriano. She holds on tight."

Cassidy tried not to blush. She absolutely failed.

"And Silvia?" she asked.

"She rides with me," Lorenzo said. "She trusts my driving."

"I do not," Silvia muttered.

"And Giacomo?" Cassidy asked.

"Driving Nonna Vivi to Brunella's bunker of safety."

"Ah."

It all made sense — chaotic sense, but still sense.

The Motorcycles Arrive

Twenty minutes later, they stood in front of two gleaming motorcycles Lorenzo had "borrowed" from acquaintances who owed him favors. Cassidy did not ask, but at first glance she could ascertain they were perfect.

Gleaming chrome.

Deep, throaty engines.

And red. Of course they were red.

The perfect shade to not attract attention while careening across the Italian countryside trying to avoid potential assassins and an organized crime gang.

But as Cassidy stood before the motorcycles, she couldn't help remembering the *last* time Adriano had taken her on a countryside ride — a day that had begun with the promise of a romantic picnic and had ended with her half-convinced the universe was actively trying to slap her for being happy. Back then, they'd raced through hills just like these, wind tangling her hair, Adriano's body warm under her hands, the world unfolding in sunlit greens and golds. He had planned a sweet, simple lunch under an oak tree... and instead they'd been ambushed by truffle hunters, attacked by a rogue picnic basket, nearly seduced by cheese that was definitely illegal in several countries, and left laughing so hard she'd cried. Adriano had told her she leaned against him like she belonged there; she told him he drove like the road owed him money. It had been wild and stupid and perfect — and for one suspended afternoon, she'd believed this impossible, maddening man might be the safest place she'd ever known.

If only *this* trip to Montaione had even a sliver of that carefree magic. Instead, the stakes now were life, death, antidotes, poison honey, and the unsettling knowledge that every scenic turn could hide a hitman with bad fashion sense.

Departure Logistics

Everyone gathered again.

Giacomo placed a gentle hand on Nonna Vivi's arm. "Ready for Brunella?"

Nonna Vivi inhaled deeply. "If she asks me to churn butter, I leave."

"She will," Giacomo said.

"Then I leave immediately."

Silvia hugged Nonna Vivi tightly. "Be safe."

"I am always safe," Nonna said. "Others are the danger."

Then she pulled Cassidy into a fierce hug.

"Find the truth," she whispered in Cassidy's ear. "Do not fear it."

Cassidy swallowed hard. "I'm not sure I like that instruction."

"You will," Nonna Vivi said. "Eventually."

Giacomo helped the older woman into a modest old car — a Fiat that looked like it prayed each time it started. Nina climbed in and took up the entire backseat. They drove off in a cloud of dust and happy barks.

Then it was the group's turn.

Lorenzo strapped two bags onto his motorcycle. "We follow the vineyards," he said. "Through Poggibonsi, Barberino, and the small hills. Scenic, quiet, fast."

Silvia climbed onto the back of his bike. "If we die," she said, "I blame you."

"If we die," he replied, "I blame the bees."

This did nothing to comfort her.

Adriano approached Cassidy. "Are you ready?"

"No," she admitted. "But since when has that stopped us?"

He gave her the kind of smile that ruined and restored her sense of self at the same time.

"Come," he said.

Cassidy climbed onto the bike behind him, wrapped her arms around his waist, and felt his laughter vibrate under her palms.

He revved the engine.

7

"Oh God," she whispered.
"Oh God," Silvia echoed.
"LET'S GO!" Lorenzo shouted.
And they launched onto the road.

The Ride to Montaione

The first curve nearly launched Cassidy's soul into the afterlife.
"LEAN WITH ME!" Adriano shouted.
"I AM LEANING!"
"You are leaning the wrong direction!"
"I DON'T KNOW WHAT I'M DOING!"
But after a few minutes, something incredible happened:
She got the hang of it.
Warm air rushed past her face, tasting like wine and sun-warmed dust.
Vineyards rose around them in elegant green waves.
Stone houses dotted the hillsides like ancient mysteries.
Olive trees sparkled silver-green as the wind brushed their leaves.
They passed through tiny villages with red-tiled roofs, laundry flapping like gossip flags, old men arguing at café tables, and Vespas buzzing like caffeinated bees.
And as they wove through those postcard-perfect villages, Cassidy felt something tug loose inside her — a small, quiet piece she rarely let herself examine. Because this, *this*, was the Italy she had imagined when she first packed her bags and stepped onto the plane: a life stitched together with slow mornings, warm evenings, and beautiful moments that didn't involve death threats or sprinting from criminals. In another version of her future — the version she still stubbornly hoped might exist — she pictured herself in a little stone cottage with peeling blue shutters, waking to the smell of fresh espresso instead of danger. She imagined buying figs from a market stall, arguing with old ladies about olive oil brands, writing ridiculous travel articles from a sunlit balcony, and hosting tiny garden dinners where Adriano grilled something scandalously

8

delicious while Lorenzo judged her wine choices. She fantasized about afternoons spent reading in hammocks, evenings spent wandering through vineyards, and nights filled with laughter instead of adrenaline. No conspiracies. No ledgers. No asphodel quests. Just a life that tasted like rosemary and sea breeze — a life where the only thing trying to kill her was her cholesterol after too much pecorino. She wanted that future so badly her chest ached... and yet here she was, wrapped around Adriano as they tore toward Montaione on a mission that seemed designed to make sure she never got it.

Every time Adriano leaned into a turn, Cassidy tightened her arms around him — not from fear anymore, but because it felt right.

They roared past stone walls and sleepy farms.

Over medieval bridges.

Down narrow roads lined with cypress trees standing like solemn guardians.

Lorenzo led confidently, Silvia clinging for dear life.

Adriano followed close.

Cassidy's heart caught in her throat more than once — in a good way.

The strange mix of terror and freedom that only Italy seemed able to conjure.

Somewhere between Siena and Montaione, she realized something:

She wasn't running anymore.

She was moving toward something — the truth, the antidote, maybe even home.

The Vineyard — One Kilometer Outside Montaione

They slowed as Lorenzo pulled off the main road and followed a narrow gravel path winding between rows of vines heavy with grapes. The vineyard sprawled across a golden hillside, bathed in late afternoon light. A stone farmhouse sat at the top, warm and welcoming. Dogs barked in greeting.

9

A man waved from the porch — broad-shouldered, bearded, wearing an apron dusted with flour.

"THAT'S ENRICO!" Lorenzo shouted.

"He looks friendly!" Cassidy called.

"He is not friendly!" Silvia corrected. "He once ordered a goat to charge at a tax inspector!"

"I WAS DEFENDING MY HONOR!" Enrico roared from the porch.

Oh good. A normal Italian man.

They rolled to a stop.

Enrico swept Lorenzo into a bear hug so powerful ribs protested audibly.

"You came back!" Enrico boomed. "And you brought... people!"

"Yes," Lorenzo said. "We need your help."

"You always do."

"We need a safe place to stay," Adriano said.

"And asphodel," Cassidy added.

Enrico's eyebrows shot up. "Ah," he said. "So you are hunting ghosts."

"Pretty much," Cassidy replied.

"Then welcome," he said, gesturing broadly. "To my vineyard of questionable decisions."

And This... Is Where Everything Goes Wrong

Because as they dismounted... as Cassidy took off her helmet... as the sun dipped and the vineyard glowed like a postcard... a muffled gunshot cracked through the air.

Then another.

Then shouting.

Then footsteps.

Adriano shoved Cassidy behind him.

Lorenzo swore.

Silvia ducked as something whizzed by her head.
Enrico yelled something about his grapes.
And just like that —
Gunshots and Gelato officially began.

Chapter 2 – Paint, Pasta, and Poor Life Choices

The first shot cracked through the air like a verdict. Cassidy's body reacted before her brain did. She flinched, heart slamming against her ribs, as a bright burst of color exploded against the stone pillar beside her and sprayed the vineyard wall in a violent splash of red. She stared at it. Not blood.

Paint.

The second shot hit Enrico square in the chest.

He staggered backward with a grunt, staring down at the vivid blue stain spreading across his apron like someone had murdered a cartoon on his torso.

For one suspended heartbeat, everyone froze.

Adriano had already shoved Cassidy behind him, hand out as if he could physically stop bullets. Lorenzo crouched low, pulling Silvia with him. Enrico looked personally insulted on a spiritual level. Somewhere out in the rows of vines—screaming.

High-pitched. Delighted. Not at all "we're committing homicide" energy.

"YOU ABSOLUTE IDIOTS!" Enrico roared in Italian, voice booming across the hillside.

People materialized from between the vines like startled woodland creatures—only these ones were wearing padded vests and cheap camouflage, masks pushed up on their heads, paintball guns dangling from their hands. A British stag party, by the look of them. Red faces, neon wristbands, one man in a plastic crown.

"Sorry, mate!" the crowned one called. "We thought this was still the field!"

"This is *my house!*" Enrico bellowed, slapping his blue-splattered chest. "This is not the *campo di guerra!* The war zone is clearly marked! There are signs! There are FLAGS!"

A skinny blond guy squinted back toward the vines. "To be fair, the sign was in Italian."

"YOU ARE IN ITALY!" Enrico thundered.

Paint dripped slowly from his apron. Cassidy's heart, which had been sprinting toward an early grave, tried to figure out what to do with itself.

She felt laughter rise in her chest, hot and hysterical. After the last twenty-four hours, she was wired for real bullets, real knives, real danger. And apparently Tuscany had decided to hit her with... British tourists playing paintball.

Silvia exhaled a shaky breath that turned into a half-sob, half-laugh. "Are you... kidding me?"

Lorenzo dragged a hand down his face. "Of course. Of course this is what happens."

Adriano glanced from the paint-splattered stone to the flock of apologetic stag-party warriors and let his shoulders drop, muscles unwinding a fraction. "Paint," he said, voice flat with disbelief.

Cassidy clung to his jacket, then let out a choked laugh she couldn't stop. "I just nearly died of a heart attack from a man named—" she squinted at one guy's novelty sash "—'Gareth the Groomzilla'."

"That is not a real title," Adriano muttered.

"It is tonight!" Gareth declared proudly, then flinched when Enrico took a step forward.

"YOU ARE OUT OF THE DESIGNATED AREA!" Enrico shouted. "The contract is very clear! You shoot each other in the lower field! Not my walls! Not my grapes! Not my guests!"

He jabbed a finger toward Cassidy and the others. "They are fragile! Emotionally compromised! I am emotionally compromised!"

Gareth lifted both hands in surrender, paintball marker dangling. "We'll, uh, head back then, yeah? Didn't mean to frighten your... family?"

Cassidy nearly choked. Enrico snapped, "They are not my family. They are worse. They are friends."

The British guys muttered apologies as they shuffled back through the rows, one of them calling, "Nice shot, though!" over his shoulder.

13

Enrico whirled on the group, chest still dripping blue. "THIS," he announced, "is why I do not rent my land to tourists. It makes them think they are allowed to exist near me."

Cassidy swallowed the last of her hysterical laughter and wiped her eyes with the back of her hand. That thin, fraying rope inside her—pulled to snapping point since Florence, since Siena, since the tunnels—loosened just a little.

They'd been dodging real bullets. Getting grazed by fake ones somehow made the whole world tilt sideways and let in a breath of absurdity she hadn't known she needed.

Lorenzo blew out a slow breath and straightened. "We're okay," he said, more to himself than anyone.

Silvia looked down at the red paint on the wall, then at her trembling hands. "I hate this country," she said. "And I never want to leave."

Adriano turned back to Cassidy. "You're not hurt?"

"No." Her voice was a little hoarse. "Just... overcooked."

"I will fix that," Enrico declared. "Inside. Now." He pointed at the guesthouse like it had insulted him. "You all look like chewed prosciutto. You need food, wine, and horizontal surfaces."

"Sleep?" Cassidy asked hopefully.

"Eventually," Enrico said. "First, we eat like people who survived war. Then you may die in bed if you insist."

Cassidy met Adriano's eyes. Something in his softened. "Go," he said quietly. "We rest tonight."

"And tomorrow?"

"Tomorrow," he said, "we save everyone else."

Enrico's Sanctuary of Starch

The guesthouse sat just beyond the main farmhouse, tucked among olive trees and climbing roses that clung desperately to old stone walls. It was a long, low building with green shutters and terracotta tiles, the kind of place Cassidy might have bookmarked on a travel

14

site in her "sometime, maybe, fantasy" folder—before her fantasies started involving antidotes and criminal empires.

Inside, the air was cool and smelled faintly of lemon, old wood, and clean linen. Three rooms. Worn but solid furniture. A long farmhouse table occupying the central common room.

"This is yours," Enrico said, dropping his arms wide as if presenting a kingdom. "Do not break anything. If you break anything, lie about it convincingly."

Cassidy ran her fingers along the back of one of the chairs. "We really can stay?"

"You are fugitives," Enrico said cheerfully. "I am a man with poor boundaries. Of course you can stay."

He clapped his hands once. "Silvia! You help me cook. Lorenzo, set the table. Adriano, go get firewood. American—"

"Cassidy," she reminded him.

"Cassidy, you sit and try not to fall apart. You look like your soul needs carbs."

Cassidy opened her mouth to protest that she could help. Her knees disagreed. She sank into a chair with a sigh she felt in her bones.

Enrico paused, then softened just a fraction. "You did good to get here," he said, quieter now. "Whatever madness you brought with you, it can sit outside for one night."

She nodded. "I'll try."

He vanished into the kitchen with Silvia on his heels.

Within minutes, the house filled with sound: the rush of water, the roll of pots, the hiss and pop of oil as something met a hot pan. Garlic hit the air first—sharp and bright—followed by onion, then the deep, round note of tomatoes cooking down, the subtle perfume of fresh basil torn by hand. Cassidy closed her eyes and let the aromas wrap around her like a blanket.

Lorenzo set plates and glasses with efficient care, stacking cutlery, unrolling napkins. Nina trotted in from their bikes, sniffed every corner like a customs officer, then collapsed under the table with a satisfied grunt.

15

Adriano returned with an armful of firewood, shirt slightly damp along the collar. Cassidy watched him for a moment—strong, tired, moving like a man who had run too far on too little—and felt something tighten in her chest that wasn't fear this time.

"You should sit," she said.

"In a minute." He crouched by the fireplace at the far end of the room, stacking logs, coaxing flames to life with practiced motions. As the fire caught, the room seemed to exhale. Shadows softened. Edges blurred. Her shoulders dropped another inch.

When the first platter arrived, Cassidy thought she might weep.

"Antipasti," Enrico announced, as if they'd won something. "You will pace yourselves or you will die."

He and Silvia set down plates laden with sliced prosciutto, salami, mortadella, wedges of pecorino and asiago, marinated artichokes, glossy black olives, grilled zucchini and eggplant, crostini smeared with chicken liver pâté and another topped with some sort of creamy, garlicky spread Cassidy didn't even need to identify before falling in love with it.

"Eat," Enrico commanded.

They obeyed.

The first bite was almost painful. Salt, fat, acid, richness—the anchoring weight of food that wasn't eaten on the run, or standing in a cellar wondering who might kill them. Cassidy's entire nervous system seemed to shudder and slowly recalibrate.

"This is obscene," she said around a mouthful of prosciutto.

"You're welcome," Enrico replied.

Pasta followed—two kinds, because apparently moderation had died sometime in the early planning stages. Wide ribbons of pappardelle tangled in a slow-cooked wild boar ragù that tasted like smoke and red wine and time; then a huge bowl of spaghetti aglio e olio, glossy with olive oil, garlic, and chili, scattered with parsley and toasted breadcrumbs.

"You made two?" Cassidy asked, incredulous.

"Of course," Enrico said. "You look like education is lacking in your life."

There was bread, too. Always bread. Crusty, rustic loaves they used to scoop up sauce, to mop plates clean, to hold in their hands like proof that they were still here.

Wine flowed easily—deep ruby Chianti that warmed Cassidy's chest and loosened her tongue. And somewhere between the second glass and the third plate of pasta, the tight knot of panic that had been living at the base of her skull started to unwind.

They talked. At first about nothing—the idiocy of paintball tourists, Brunella's rumored ability to turn grown men into obedient schoolboys, Nina's clear belief that she deserved a personal chair at the table. But eventually, inevitably, the conversation turned toward the thing that had driven them here.

A Mad Recap Over Wine

"So," Enrico said, topping up everyone's glasses. "Start from the beginning. Why do men with bad suits and worse attitudes want my friend dead this time?"

Lorenzo leaned back, swirling his wine. "You remember Giulia," he said. "My stepmother."

Enrico's expression darkened. "Of course. The genius. The storm. The one who made vinegar that made people cry."

"That one," Adriano murmured.

"She discovered something," Silvia said. "About the honey trade. About Davide."

Enrico snorted. "Davide. I should have poisoned him when I had the chance."

"You didn't have the chance," Lorenzo said.

"I would have made the chance."

Cassidy smiled faintly despite herself.

"She found out they were tainting honey," Adriano continued. "Slow poison. Subtle. Spread wide. And trying to stop it got her killed."

Enrico's jaw clenched.

17

"And now," Cassidy added quietly, fingers brushing the ledger resting near her plate, "we've discovered my mother was part of the same fight. She was working with a group—the Keepers—to keep the sweetness clean. She left this for me. A recipe. An antidote."

"And Davide wants it gone," Silvia said.

"And wants us gone," Lorenzo added.

Enrico looked between them all, eyes flicking to the fire, to the window, to the vineyard outside as if tracing lines only he could see. "So you go from Florence to Siena," he said slowly, "from Nonna's kidnapping to tunnels beneath the city, to some theatrical showdown at the fountain—"

"Approximate," Silvia said.

"—and then you come here," he finished, "to find a flower that may or may not exist."

"Asphodel exists," Lorenzo said. "It's just shy."

"It's a plant," Enrico said. "It is not shy. It is lazy."

Cassidy laughed, the sound edged with exhaustion. "We only need enough to make a batch of antidote. We can test it, confirm it works, then... I don't know. Scale it up. Get it into the supply. Stop the damage."

"They won't let you do that easily," Enrico said.

"Nothing has been easy so far," Adriano replied.

Enrico studied them one by one—the tired determination in Adriano's face, the stubborn fire in Cassidy's eyes, Silvia's sharp intelligence, Lorenzo's strange mix of grief and humor. He sighed, then nodded once, as if making peace with something.

"Then we do it my way," he said. "You stay here. You eat until your souls come back into your bodies. You sleep. And tomorrow we start hunting flowers and cooking revenge."

"Cooking revenge," Cassidy repeated. "That's going on a T-shirt someday."

"I'll design it," Lorenzo said.

Dance It Off

18

By the time the second bottle of wine died a noble death and the last smear of ragù had been wiped from the last plate, Cassidy's limbs felt pleasantly heavy. Enrico cleared the table with military efficiency while Silvia shooed everyone away from the dishes with the ferocity of a woman who'd chosen her post.

"You saved us," she said, stacking plates. "The least we can do is not be useless guests."

"You are always useless guests," Enrico said. "It is your charm."

As he retreated, he flicked on an old stereo in the corner. Music flooded the room—something jazzy, old, Italian, the kind of song that could play behind any scene in any movie set in Tuscany and feel exactly right.

Cassidy leaned back in her chair and let herself sink into the moment. The fire crackled. The wine glowed in the glass. Lorenzo tapped a rhythm on the table, shoulders moving. Nina snored underfoot.

"You look almost happy," Adriano said quietly beside her.

She turned her head to look at him. The firelight softened the hard edges that had carved into his face over the last days. He looked older. And younger. And entirely, dangerously beautiful.

"I forgot what happy felt like," she said honestly. "This is a decent reminder."

Lorenzo stood abruptly and held out a hand to Silvia. "Dance with me."

"No," she said on reflex.

He tilted his head. "Dance with me anyway."

She hesitated just long enough for him to grin, then she sighed and slid her hand into his. "One," she warned. "One song. If you try to spin me, I will vomit on your shoes."

"That is a risk I am willing to take."

He pulled her into the open space near the fire, and they began to move. Not gracefully. Not at first. Lorenzo exaggerated the rhythms, Silvia stumbled, laughed, and swatted his shoulder. But the second chorus hit, and something clicked. They spun—not showy, not expert, but relaxed, alive. For once, nobody was chasing them. Nobody was shooting. Nobody was yelling except Enrico from the kitchen, complaining about a pan.

Cassidy watched them and felt an odd pulse behind her ribs, something like hope and grief tangled together.

Adriano's fingers brushed her wrist. "We could dance too."

"We could," she said. "But we both know you'd be too good at it and it would be embarrassing."

His mouth curved. "You don't like me being good at things?"

"I like you being good at things where I can still pretend I have the upper hand."

He leaned in a fraction closer. "You always have the upper hand."

"You're lying."

"Yes," he admitted. "Completely."

Her laugh caught at the edges of something else—something warm and slightly terrifying.

Enrico emerged with a tray of tiny glasses sloshing with pale golden liquid. "Limóncello!" he announced. "For digestion. Also for bad decisions."

"Perfect," Cassidy said, accepting a glass.

They clinked. They drank. The lemon liqueur burned and soothed at the same time; sugar and sting. The room blurred just enough to dull the sharp edges of reality.

Song after song rolled on. Lorenzo and Silvia traded places. At one point, Enrico tried to dance with Cassidy. Cassidy was unconvinced. Adriano did eventually pull Cassidy to her feet, and they swayed in a small circle near the window. She let her forehead rest against his chest and listened to his heartbeat, steady under all the noise.

For a precious, suspended sliver of night, everything else—the ledger, the poison, Davide's shadow—felt far away.

Morning, Messages, and Reality

The morning hit harder than any bullet. Light knifed in through the shutters, slicing across the rustic wardrobe, the cracked plaster walls, the tangle of sheets twisted around Cassidy's legs. Her mouth tasted like wine and lemon and bad choices. Her head felt like someone had stuffed it with cotton.

For a few gorgeous seconds, she didn't remember why they were here. There was just the scent of Enrico's coffee drifting up from somewhere downstairs, the soft creak of the house stretching awake, and Adriano's arm heavy across her waist.

Then it all came back.

She cracked one eye open. Adriano lay on his side, face relaxed in sleep, the usual lines of worry smoothed away. His hand rested at her hip, warm and possessive even unconscious.

A sharp ping shattered the quiet.

Adriano's phone, abandoned on the bedside table, lit up.

He flinched awake; Cassidy groaned and flopped an arm over her face. "Tell whoever that is to go away," she mumbled. "We're dead."

"Not yet," he said, voice rough with sleep. He reached for the phone, squinting at the screen. His expression shifted. "It's from Giacomo."

That cut through the fog.

Cassidy pushed herself up, sheet pulling around her. "Nonna?"

Adriano read quickly, then exhaled. Some of the tension that had already started to creep back into his body loosened. "They're safe," he said. "At Brunella's. He says the house is 'fortified with saints and curses.'"

"That sounds right," Cassidy said. Relief flooded her so fast she felt dizzy.

"He also says," Adriano added, "that Brunella has already tried to feed him to death."

"That also sounds right."

Adriano showed her the screen. A blurry photo of Nonna Vivi sitting at a massive wooden table, scowling at the camera, a plate

21

piled high with food in front of her. Nina's head lurked at the edge of the frame, eyes fixed on the plate with religious devotion.

Underneath: *We are alive. Eat. Rest. Do not be stupid. – G.*

Cassidy smiled, throat tightening. "Too late on the stupid part," she murmured.

Adriano set the phone down and leaned his head back against the wall. "They're safe," he repeated. "For now."

The "for now" sat between them. Heavy. Inevitable.

"Do you think Davide has any idea how close we are?" she asked.

"I think he suspects," Adriano said. "If he didn't before Siena, he does now."

"Then people are still being poisoned."

He closed his eyes briefly. "Yes."

There it was again—the guilt, the urgency, the gnawing helplessness. Cassidy felt it clawing at the edges of her calm like a tide trying to drag her out to sea.

"No," she said, surprising herself with the force in her voice.

Adriano looked at her.

"We can't do that to ourselves," she said. "Not yet. Not now. If we don't rest, we're useless. If we spiral, we're useless. We know the clock is ticking, but we finally have what we need to stop it."

"The ledger," he said.

"The ledger," she echoed.

He studied her for a moment longer, then nodded. "We work today," he said. "But first, coffee."

"God, yes."

They dressed—slowly—and made their way downstairs, where Enrico had indeed already summoned coffee and breakfast like some benevolent domestic warlord. Silvia sat at the table with her head in her hands, hair a mess, a mug clutched between both palms as if it were preventing her from evaporating. Lorenzo looked unfairly functional, scrolling his phone and pretending not to smirk at her misery.

"You look awful," he told Cassidy cheerfully.

22

"Thank you," she said. "It's called surviving."
"You look better than she does," he added, nodding at Silvia.
"I will murder you," Silvia said into her coffee.
"Not before coffee," Enrico said, slapping a plate of toast and jam down in front of her. "Murder requires fuel."
They ate—simple things this time. Toast, jam, yogurt, fruit, slices of cheese. Enrico insisted they drink water between coffees "so your organs do not weep later." The normalcy of it all made Cassidy's chest ache.
When the worst of the fog lifted and the second round of espresso hit, Lorenzo pushed his chair back. "We should start," he said.
Adriano nodded. "Where?"
"The kitchen," Enrico said. "Where else do you make miracles?"

Beginning the Antidote

Enrico's kitchen was both chaos and cathedral. Pans hung from the ceiling. Jars lined the shelves—honey, vinegar, spices, mysterious preserves that glowed like captured sunsets. A large window overlooked the vineyard, morning light pouring in and pooling on the wide wooden worktable.
Cassidy set the ledger down in the center like an offering. Adriano stood at her left, Lorenzo at her right. Silvia leaned against the counter, arms crossed, eyes sharp. Enrico hovered near the stove, pretending not to care while very obviously caring.
Cassidy opened to the page they'd studied in Siena: *Ricetta Antidoto—Primavera.*
Her mother's handwriting curled across the paper. Other hands had added notes in the margins. Ratios. Temperatures. Latin names of plants she still couldn't pronounce.
"We start with the base," Lorenzo said. "Chestnut honey, acacia honey, vinegar madre, propolis, royal jelly."

23

"That we have," Enrico said, moving to his shelves.
He gathered jars like a conjurer assembling ingredients for a spell: dark, almost bitter chestnut honey; pale liquid acacia honey that caught the light; a heavy bottle of cloudy, living vinegar; a small container of propolis, resinous and strange; a tiny jar of royal jelly that Enrico cradled like a relic.

"This is expensive," he said. "If you waste it, I disown all of you."

"You don't own us," Silvia pointed out.

"Correct," he said. "I upgrade that to: I will haunt you."

They measured carefully, following the ratios in the ledger. Cassidy read; Adriano stirred; Lorenzo weighed ingredients with a precision that would make a chemist proud. As they worked, the kitchen filled with a complex scent—sweet, sharp, earthy, almost metallic at the back of the tongue.

"The bitter agent," Silvia murmured. "That's what we're fighting."

"We balance it," Lorenzo said. "Bind it. Neutralize it."

Cassidy's finger traced a margin note in her mother's quick script. *If taste lingers bitter, add asphodel infusion. Field-tested, Montaione hills.*

Her chest squeezed. "She really was here," she said softly. "In this region. Hunting the same flower. Fighting the same fight."

"And now you finish it," Adriano said.

They worked through the morning—careful, focused. The act of following the recipe gave Cassidy something solid to cling to. Step by step. Stir, heat, cool, taste. Adjust. It felt like journalism in a way: research, assemble, refine, reveal. Only this story could end with people living or dying.

By midday, they stood over a small jar of thick, amber liquid that glowed faintly in the light.

"This is the base," Lorenzo said. "Without asphodel, it's incomplete. It might help. It might not be enough."

"We won't know until we test it," Adriano said.

"Which we are not doing on ourselves," Silvia added quickly.

"Obviously," Lorenzo said.

Enrico cleared his throat. "You will not poison my chickens either," he said. "I am grown man, I can buy my own antidotes."
A quiet settled over them. The jar sat between them like a promise —and a challenge.
"So," Cassidy said finally. "Next step."
"Asphodel," Adriano said.
"Tomorrow," Lorenzo added. "Today, we rest the rest of the way. If we go up into the hills exhausted, the flowers will laugh at us."
Cassidy snorted. "I hate that that makes sense."
It did, though. Her body ached. Her brain buzzed. The wine from last night hadn't fully relinquished its hold. They needed to be sharp for whatever came next.
"Tonight," Enrico said, "you eat light, you drink less, and you go to bed early."
Everyone glanced at Cassidy and Adriano.
Enrico narrowed his eyes. "TRY," he said.

Moonlight and Momentum

The moon rose late, full and bright, washing the vineyard in silver. The wind had quieted; crickets sang; the house creaked softly as it settled into the night. Cassidy stood at the window of their room, one hand on the rough stone of the sill, looking out over the rows of vines. From up here, the world looked almost gentle. The crisis felt like something that could be solved in the space of a night, as if dawn might somehow bring a miracle.

Footsteps behind her. Adriano, freshly showered, hair still damp, moving quietly so as not to disturb the illusion of peace.

"Can't sleep?" he asked.

She didn't turn. "Can't stop thinking."

"About?"

She huffed a soft laugh. "Pick one. Davide. The poisoned honey. The asphodel. My mother. Nonna Vivi. The possibility of dying in a field tomorrow because a flower gets offended we showed up without a bottle of wine."

25

He came to stand beside her, shoulder brushing hers as he looked out. "Fair."

The silence between them was comfortable now, threaded through with exhaustion and something much hungrier. The last days had pulled them tight, wound them together with fear and urgency. Tonight, for the first time in what felt like years, that tension had space to stretch into something else.

"You know," Cassidy said quietly, "when I imagined Italy before I came here, I pictured nights like this. Moonlight, vineyards, maybe a little melancholy from too much wine. Not... this." She gestured vaguely, encompassing criminal syndicates and biochemical sabotage.

"What did you imagine?" Adriano asked.

She hesitated. "Simple things. Waking up slow. Coffee in bed. Maybe writing something that didn't involve death. Having dinner with the same people so often that the waiter knew our order. Arguing about dessert. Going to bed knowing that tomorrow would probably look a lot like today." She swallowed. "I thought that would be boring. Now it sounds like a miracle."

He watched her for a long moment, something softening in his gaze. "We could still have that," he said.

She almost laughed, but the earnestness in his voice stopped her. "We're kind of in over our heads at the moment, in case you hadn't noticed."

"After," he said. "After we finish this. After we stop him. There can be an 'after.'"

"Big talk for a man who just stirred an antidote like it was a risotto," she said.

He smiled faintly. "I am excellent at risotto."

"I know," she said, and the warmth in her voice surprised them both.

His hand brushed hers on the windowsill. She didn't pull away. Neither did he.

The air between them thickened—charged, heavy with things unsaid and too many things said under duress. Cassidy felt her pulse pick up for reasons that had nothing to do with fear.

"You scared me yesterday," he said softly.

She blinked. "With what? My limoncello intake?"

"When the paintball hit the wall." His jaw worked. "For a moment I thought—"

"I know," she said. "Me too."

He turned toward her fully then, leaning a hip against the sill, close enough that she could see the tiny scar near his eyebrow, the faint trace of stubble he hadn't bothered to shave. Close enough that the heat of his body brushed her skin.

"We keep almost dying," he said. "And every time we don't, I... feel something. Stronger."

"Trauma bonding," she supplied lightly.

He gave her a look. "No. You know that's not what this is."

She did. She'd known it for a while now. Since the first time he'd looked at her like she was both a problem and a solution. Since he'd trusted her with his grief, his anger, his grandmother. Since they'd stood in Siena's tunnels with danger closing in and kissed like drowning people sharing air.

Her voice dropped. "What is it then?"

His hand slid from the windowsill to her waist, fingers resting lightly at her hip. He moved slowly, giving her all the time in the world to step back. She didn't.

"It's you," he said simply. "Being here. Still being here. After everything."

She swallowed hard. "You're here too."

"I have been here," he said. "In Italy. In this house, that kitchen, these hills. But I was not... here." He touched his chest with his free hand. "Not really. Not since Giulia died."

Her throat tightened. She reached up, fingers brushing the side of his neck. His pulse jumped under her touch.

"You make it feel like I could be again," he said.

The honesty in his voice almost hurt.

She stepped closer, closing the last inches between them. Her free hand slid up to cup his jaw. "And you," she said, "make it feel like I didn't come here just to run away."

He bent his head, slowly, as if giving her time to change her mind. She didn't. Their mouths met—soft at first, then deeper, hungrier. Heat surged through her, immediate and overwhelming. She curled her fingers into his hair and felt him inhale sharply against her lips.

The kiss shifted, gathering force. The hand at her hip tightened, pulling her closer; her body slotted against his, instinctive and right. She parted her lips; he took the invitation, kissing her with a kind of desperate gentleness that made her knees weak. She broke away just for a breath, foreheads touching, their breaths mingling in the narrow space between them.

"We shouldn't," she whispered, though even she wasn't sure what argument she was making.

"We should," he countered, equally soft.

"We're exhausted. We're half-drunk. We're—"

"Alive," he said. "We're alive, Cassidy."

Something in her uncoiled completely.

She kissed him again, harder this time, and felt him answer with a low sound in his throat that sent a shiver down her spine. He walked her backward from the window, slow, careful, as if each step was a question she could still say no to. Her legs bumped the edge of the bed; she sat, dragging him with her by his shirt.

They moved together, guided more by instinct than thought, shedding the day like a too-heavy coat. His hands were sure and reverent, tracing the lines of her back, her shoulders, her hips as if memorizing a map. Her fingers wandered over his chest, his arms, feeling the tension and strength there, the scars time and grief had left.

It was not the frantic, adrenaline-fueled collision of Siena's tunnels. It was slower, deeper, heat rising between them in waves.

Every kiss, every touch said the same thing: *we're still here, we're still here, we're still here.*

The moonlight spilled across the bed in a pale stripe, painting their skin in silver and shadow. Outside, the vineyard slept. Inside, the world narrowed to the slide of his mouth on hers, the warmth of his body, the low murmur of her name like a prayer he was afraid to say too loud.

She lost track of time. Of words. Of anything except the way he made her feel—unraveled and held together all at once, like something fragile and indestructible at the same time.

When they finally stilled, tangled in the sheets, breath coming in uneven waves, the moon had shifted higher. Adriano's arm curled around her again, pulling her close against his chest. She rested her head there, listening to his heartbeat gradually slow, matching her own.

They lay there in the quiet, the night wrapped around them.

Cassidy stared at the pale stripe of moonlight on the ceiling and felt a strange, fierce calm settle over her. Tomorrow there would be flowers to find, poisons to counter, enemies to face. Tomorrow the world would be sharp and dangerous again.

But tonight, in this small room above a vineyard of questionable decisions, she had this: warmth, breath, the solid weight of him beside her, the knowledge that somehow, against all odds, they'd made it this far.

She closed her eyes.

For the first time in a very long time, Cassidy Moore fell asleep not running from something, but moving toward it.

Chapter 3 – Asphodel and Other Bad Omens

Morning arrived with the stubborn optimism of a place that refused to acknowledge crime syndicates. Sunlight poured over the hills, spreading gold across the vineyard rows and slipping through the slats of the shutters in thin, bright lines. Birds shouted their opinions from the cypress trees. Somewhere below, Enrico was already yelling at a tractor.

Cassidy woke slowly, surfacing through layers of sleep and exhaustion to the faint aroma of coffee, warm bread, and woodsmoke. For a few seconds, she lay still, eyes closed, trying to catalogue the sensations.

Soft mattress.

Cool sheet tangled around her legs.

A pleasant ache in her muscles that had nothing to do with running for her life.

The steady warmth at her back—Adriano, breathing evenly, arm draped around her waist like he no longer trusted the universe to keep her where he'd left her.

Reality trickled back in. Siena. The ledger. The antidote base they'd mixed yesterday. Davide. Poisoned honey. Nonna Vivi at Brunella's fortress of saints and curses. Asphodel.

She sighed and rolled carefully onto her back.

Adriano's eyes were already open, watching her. "Buongiorno," he murmured.

"Creepy," she said softly. "But also kind of nice."

He smiled, the slow, small one that pulled more at one corner of his mouth. "You were frowning in your sleep."

"That tracks." She scrubbed a hand over her face. "Did we… sleep at all?"

"For a little while," he said. "Enough to remember what it feels like."

She thought of the previous night—the heat, the hungry tenderness, the way they'd clung to each other as if the world

30

might vanish if they let go. Then they had finally, actually slept, limbs tangled, breath synced.

The memory warmed her even as the weight of the day settled on her chest.

"Asphodel," she said.

"Asphodel," he agreed.

She rolled to face him. "Be honest. How likely is it that today turns into yet another near-death experience?"

He considered. "On a scale of one to ten?"

"Yes."

He hesitated. "Eight."

"That's higher than yesterday."

"Yesterday began with cleaning off paint," he pointed out.

"Okay, fair." She exhaled. "Then we'd better get coffee."

Coffee, Curses, and a Plan

They found Lorenzo and Silvia already at the farmhouse table, looking in various stages of human. Lorenzo was mostly put together — hair damp from a recent shower, shirt fresh, eyes clear with the annoying resilience of someone who metabolized wine like water. Silvia, by contrast, had her hair in an approximate bun and her face buried in a mug.

"How are we alive?" Cassidy muttered as she slid into a chair.

"We're not," Silvia said without lifting her head. "This is a pre-death hallucination."

Enrico swept in from the kitchen carrying a new moka pot of coffee like it was a sacred artifact. "You are all dramatic," he announced. "You had food, you had sleep, you had wine, you had… whatever that was last night." He flicked a meaningful glance between Cassidy and Adriano. "Some of us had to listen to floorboards."

Cassidy felt her face heat. Adriano's did too, though he masked it by reaching for the coffee.

"Thin floors," Enrico continued. "Very thin. Think about that before you shout each other's names at midnight."

Lorenzo choked on his coffee. Silvia's head snapped up, eyes suddenly wide awake and very, very entertained.

"We were not—" Cassidy started, then realized there was no version of that sentence that didn't make everything worse. "I'm going to drown myself in espresso."

"Good," Enrico said. "You will need energy. Today, you go up into the hills. We find your flower. We try not to get shot by tourists."

"That's our baseline now?" Silvia said. "Try not to get shot?"

"By tourists," Enrico clarified. "If professionals shoot at you, they will at least respect your time."

Cassidy took a long gulp of coffee, letting the bitterness anchor her. "What's the plan?" she asked, once her dignity had finished dying.

Lorenzo pushed his plate away and spread the ledger out between the crumbs. "We mapped it out last night while you two were… rearranging the furniture."

"Lorenzo," Adriano said in warning.

"I am just saying," Lorenzo replied, unapologetic. "Some chairs are not where I left them."

"Focus," Silvia cut in, though her smirk gave her away.

Lorenzo tapped a hand-drawn map tucked into the back of the ledger—his additions to Cassidy's mother's neat lines and notes. "My mother Giulia and your mother both used these hills," he said to Cassidy. "Here, here, and here." He pointed to three shaded areas around Montaione. "My friend from the foraging group says asphodel grows most densely in this zone—north slope, near the old shepherd paths."

"Is this the same friend who thinks nettles are a snack?" Silvia asked.

"He is a man of complex tastes."

"And is anyone else looking for asphodel?" Adriano asked. "Recently?"

Lorenzo's mouth tightened. "He said people have been asking. New faces. Men with city shoes."

"City shoes?" Cassidy repeated.

"Soles not made for mud," Lorenzo said. "Men who don't know how to walk around a thistle. Davide's people, probably. Or his clients."

The coffee soured slightly in Cassidy's stomach. "So we're racing them to the flowers."

"Essentially." Lorenzo folded the map. "Which is why we take only who we need today. Less noise. Less attention."

"Who's going?" Cassidy asked, though she already knew.

"Me, you, Adriano," Lorenzo said. "And the dog."

"Obviously the dog," Silvia murmured.

"What about you?" Cassidy asked her.

"I stay here and pretend to be responsible," Silvia replied. "Someone has to talk to Giacomo if he calls. Or run interference if Davide's people sniff around."

"I can help," Enrico said. "I will tell them you all left at dawn for Rome to confess your sins."

"You go to Rome to confess your sins?" Cassidy asked.

"Big sins," Enrico said. "Small ones you confess to the your nonna, then she beats them out of you with focaccia."

"That tracks," Lorenzo muttered.

"So." Cassidy looked at the ledger, then at the window, where the morning light had climbed to a more assertive angle. "We hike. We search. We try not to be seen. We gather asphodel. We come back and play potions."

"We do not call it potions," Adriano said automatically.

"We absolutely call it potions," she countered.

His mouth twitched. "Fine. We play potions."

Enrico nodded briskly. "Eat. Then go. The hills do not wait."

Cassidy buttered a slice of toast with more force than strictly necessary. Her body hummed with a mixture of nerves and determination. Out there, somewhere on those sunlit slopes, was a plant her mother had worked with. The same hills had felt Giulia's footsteps. Today would be the first time all three women's paths overlapped in one place—even if two of them only in memory and ink.

"Let's go meet the flower," she said.

Deep Into the Hillside

By mid-morning, the air had warmed enough to turn the walk into a steady sweat. They left the vineyard behind—Enrico standing on the porch, arms crossed, shouting last-minute instructions about hydration and not dying—as they followed a narrow dirt path up into the hills. Nina trotted ahead, tail high, occasionally turning to make sure her humans were keeping up. Lorenzo carried a small pack with jars, scissors, and a trowel. Adriano had slung a canteen over one shoulder, a coil of rope over the other, his movements that of a man who knew how quickly a peaceful walk could turn into something else. Cassidy kept pace between them, the ledger map folded in her back pocket.

The landscape unfolded around them in layers: vineyards giving way to scrubby grass, then small stands of oak and chestnut, the air cooling slightly as they climbed. Wildflowers dotted the path in bursts of color—poppies, daisies, clover. Bees stitched lazy paths between blossoms.

"If you were a stubborn medicinal flower hiding from criminals, where would you be?" Cassidy asked, more to the landscape than anyone.

"Somewhere inconvenient," Adriano replied.

"So: everywhere," she said.

They followed an old shepherd trail that snaked along the side of the hill, sometimes barely more than a faint depression in the grass. Birdsong echoed in the distance. A warm breeze pushed the scent of sun-baked earth and crushed herbs into their faces.

34

"This is the part of your job I do not understand," Lorenzo said, stepping over a rock. "You run toward danger. You volunteer for this."

"Which part of my job do you think this is?" Cassidy asked.

"You investigate," he said. "You chase stories."

"Most of my stories used to be about the ten best places to eat pastries without judgment," she said. "Not global poisoning schemes."

"You're very adaptable," he said.

"Trauma will do that," she replied lightly.

They walked in companionable silence for a while after that, each lost in their own thoughts. Cassidy thought about her mother's notebook—the precise handwriting, the margin notes, the way she'd written *For Cassidy* at the top of the antidote page as if she'd somehow known her daughter would someday stand in this very spot, hunting the same bloom.

She wondered if her mother had been afraid when she'd walked these hills. Or if, like Giulia, she had simply been furious.

"Here," Lorenzo said at last, pointing ahead. "See?"

They crested a small rise, and the terrain shifted again. The hill flattened into a broad, gently sloping plateau scattered with rocks and low shrubs. The soil here was paler, dusted with chalky white. And amid the scrub and stone, pale green shoots rose in clumps, topped with tall, slender flower spikes bearing clusters of delicate white petals streaked with faint pink.

Asphodel.

"It's... pretty," Cassidy said softly.

"And dangerous," Adriano added.

"Like half the people we know," she said.

Lorenzo crouched by one of the clumps, examining it closely. "This is it," he confirmed. "Asphodelus albus. Right timing, too. Young enough to be potent, old enough to give us what we need." He glanced up at Cassidy. "Your mother had good taste in plants."

Cassidy didn't trust herself to answer.

35

Enrico's dog moved ahead, nose working, as if checking the perimeter. Her ears flicked. She snuffled at a patch a few meters away, then sneezed and backed off, whining softly.

"What is it, ragazza?" Adriano asked, approaching her.

Cassidy followed, stomach tightening.

The patch the dog had investigated looked different. The plants there were stunted, leaves bruised, some of the stalks broken. A faint chemical tang hung in the air, beneath the honest scents of earth and growth.

Lorenzo frowned and crouched again, touching a leaf gently with the back of his fingers. "This is wrong," he said. "Somebody sprayed something. Or spilled."

Cassidy's heartbeat picked up. "Davide?"

"Or someone who works for him," Adriano said quietly.

Lorenzo straightened and scanned the area more carefully. Now that Cassidy was looking, she saw more signs: boot prints in the dust, too heavy and deep to be from a single passing farmer; a cigarette butt crushed into the soil; the faint impression of something having rested there—a crate, maybe, or a portable tank.

"They were here," Lorenzo murmured. "Recently."

"And they don't want anyone else getting use out of the asphodel," Cassidy said. "They're salting the earth."

"Not all of it," Adriano pointed out. "Look." He gestured to the farther reaches of the plateau, where more clumps of asphodel swayed in the breeze, untouched.

"They didn't have time to ruin everything," Lorenzo said. "Or they didn't find all the patches. This hill is wide. They would have had to work in a grid."

"We work faster," Cassidy said. "We take what we need now. Before they come back with more boots and more chemicals."

Lorenzo nodded. "We move."

They spread out slightly—still within sight of each other, but covering more ground. Lorenzo demonstrated the best way to harvest: cutting certain stems, leaving enough of the plant to regrow; taking care not to bruise the bulbs they needed for infusion.

Cassidy worked carefully, mimicking his motions, her focus narrowing to the rhythm of snip, gather, place in the jar. The air hummed with bees and the faint rustle of leaves.

She had just filled her third jar when she heard the dog growl. She looked up sharply.

The dog stood at the far edge of the plateau, hackles raised, stance stiff. Her gaze wasn't on the ground this time, but on the line of trees beyond the asphodel field, where shadow pooled more densely.

"Adriano," Cassidy called. "Lorenzo."

They both turned. Adriano moved toward the dog, slow and deliberate; Lorenzo straightened, eyes narrowing as he followed the dog's line of sight.

For a moment, the trees were just trees.

Then a figure stepped out from between them.

The Woman from the Hills

It was not a thug. Not a paintball tourist. Not a man in a cheap suit.

She was small and wiry, with sun-browned skin and hair pulled back in a gray-streaked braid. She wore sturdy boots, well-worn trousers, and a flannel shirt rolled up to her elbows. A long walking stick rested easily in one hand. She looked like she could outwalk a goat.

The dog's growl subsided into a wary whine. The woman eyed the dog, then the humans, then the jars of asphodel at their feet.

"You're not from here," she said in Italian, voice rough as gravel. Her gaze lingered on Cassidy and the ledger peeking from her back pocket. "But you're also not the other ones."

"The other ones?" Lorenzo asked, raising his hands slightly to show they were empty. "Mi scusi, signora. We don't mean any harm. We're just... harvesting."

37

"I can see that," she said dryly. Her eyes flicked to the damaged patch. "And I can see what the others did."

"Who?" Cassidy asked, switching to Italian, the words rusty but good enough. "The men who were here before?"

The woman snorted. "They weren't men. They were wolves in idiot clothing. City wolves. Heavy feet. Loud." She tapped the ground. "They came two days ago. Big car on the lower road. Up here with cans and sprayers, walking like they were going to war with plants. They asked questions about the asphodel. Offered money. I told them to go to hell. They tried to take what they wanted anyway."

"What happened?" Adriano asked.

She lifted her chin. "I told them the hill doesn't belong to cowards. Then I threw a rock at one of their heads and let my dogs chase them down the slope."

Cassidy blinked. "You... what?"

The corner of the woman's mouth twitched. "They screamed like children. One of them lost a shoe. I left it by the path as a warning."

Lorenzo made a strangled noise that might have been admiration. "We should introduce her to Brunella," he muttered to Cassidy. "If they join forces, Davide is finished."

The woman's gaze sharpened. "You know Davide?"

"We... know of him," Adriano said carefully.

Something in his tone made her nod. "Then you're not on his side."

"Very much not," Cassidy said.

"How can you tell?" Lorenzo asked her.

She rolled her eyes. "Because you know his name and you say it like you swallowed bad wine. The other ones didn't even dare say who they worked for. That's how you know a man is dangerous — when his dogs are too afraid to say his name."

Silence stretched for a heartbeat.

38

"We're trying to stop him," Cassidy said. "He's using the honey supply. Poisoning it. We have a way to fight back, but we need this." She nodded toward the flowers. "We only take what we need. We won't damage the hillside."

The woman studied her for a long moment, measuring something invisible.

"What's your name?" she finally asked.

"Cassidy. Cassidy Moore."

"Foreign."

"Yes."

"Stubborn."

"Also yes."

The woman shifted her attention to Adriano. "And you?"

"Adriano Vitale."

"And you."

"Lorenzo Bianchi."

She grunted, as if that confirmed something. "I am Marta," she said. "My family has grazed sheep on these slopes since before your mothers were born. Before Davide started playing king with other people's food." She tapped a boot against the dirt. "The hill is old. Older than the men who think they own it. It doesn't like them."

"Does it like us?" Cassidy asked.

"We'll see," Marta said. "But you have a dog with good instincts, and you didn't start by offering me money, so that's something."

She strode past them to kneel by a healthy patch of asphodel, examining the stems. Then she sniffed the air, nose wrinkling toward the damaged section.

"They tried to ruin it," she said. "Sprayed something bitter. But they don't know the hill like I do." She straightened. "If they had more time, they'd have done worse. You were lucky."

"Lucky," Cassidy repeated faintly. "That's… a word for it."

Marta squinted at the jars. "You have enough for a potion."

"Antidote," Adriano corrected automatically.

"Potion," she insisted. "All medicine is potions. Doctors just don't like that the witches knew it first."

"I like her," Lorenzo whispered.

Marta turned that hawk-bright gaze on him. "You stay away from the lower slope," she warned. "They marked trees there. Don't know for what. Maybe to find their way back. Maybe to put something there later. Either way, it's theirs now. Let the hill scrub it clean for a while."

"Marked how?" Cassidy asked.

"Red wax on the bark," Marta said. "Like blood that doesn't drip. Ugly." Her eyes went flinty. "You see that mark, you turn around. You tell people you trust. Anyone else, you pretend you're a stupid tourist who got lost."

"Is there anyone we can trust up here?" Adriano asked.

Marta considered. "Most of the old families. A few of the new ones. Not the ones who drive too-clean cars or have too-white sneakers." She jerked her chin toward the trees. "And if you see the wolves again, you tell them this hill belongs to Marta, and she is watching."

"Will that scare them?" Cassidy asked.

"No," Marta said. "But it will confuse them. Confusion is useful."

She turned to go, then paused. "You said honey," she remarked. "But he's not just touching honey."

Cassidy's skin prickled. "What do you mean?"

"Men like Davide don't stop with one thing," Marta said. "They start with what's sweet and easy. Then they go where the money is. Wine. Oil. Grain. People." Her jaw tightened. "Keep your eyes open. If you're only looking at honey, you're already behind."

Cassidy swallowed. "Thank you."

Marta shrugged, already blending back into the trees. "Don't thank me yet," she said. "Just don't waste what you're doing. The hill doesn't give second chances."

Then she was gone.

Nina stopped growling and wagged her tail once, as if to say: approved.

"Well," Lorenzo exhaled. "That was comforting in a terrifying way."

"She's right," Adriano said quietly. "We've been focused on honey. But Davide—"

"Is building a bigger web," Cassidy finished. "We knew that on some level. Oils, vinegars, exports. But hearing it from a woman who throws rocks at his employees really drives it home."

"First things first," Lorenzo said, tapping a jar. "We get the asphodel back. Make the antidote. Test it. Then we see how far his poison goes."

"Agreed," Adriano said.

Cassidy glanced once more at the damaged patch, at the faint chemical scorch in the soil. Then she bent to gather the last of the blooms. The hill, at least in this corner, had chosen them over the wolves.

They started back down.

A Hill That Bites Back

The return trip should have been easier.

They followed a different path—one of Marta's suggestions, a more sheltered route that skirted the lower slope she'd warned about. The air had warmed into proper afternoon, cicadas buzzing in the trees. Nina trotted ahead, tongue lolling, occasionally darting off the path to sniff some invisible thing.

Cassidy's shoulders began to ache under the constant tension of watching and listening for threats. Every rustle in the undergrowth sounded like footsteps. Every flash of color in the corner of her eye

41

turned into a possible jacket before her brain corrected it to "flower" or "bird."

"We're jumpy," she said finally.

"We've earned it," Adriano replied.

The trail narrowed, hugging the hillside with a drop to one side screened by shrubs. Lorenzo checked the map, then pointed ahead. "Just around this bend," he said. "We'll hit the old mule road and then it's an easy walk down to the vineyard."

"Define 'easy,'" Cassidy said.

"Less likely to fall to your death," he answered.

"That's oddly specific."

He smiled, then suddenly froze, hand shooting out.

"Wait," he said.

They stopped.

The dog had, too, a few meters ahead, body rigid, nose testing the air. Her ears went back—not in fear, but in wary calculation.

Then Cassidy heard it—a low rumble under the surface hum of summer. Not thunder. Not an engine. Something more subtle. A tremor she felt in her boots.

She looked up in time to see a trickle of small stones skid down the slope ahead, bouncing across the path.

"Rockfall," Adriano said, already moving. "Back. Move back —"

The world shifted.

The hillside above the bend shuddered, then gave way in a sudden, cascading slide of dirt, rocks, and tangled roots. It wasn't a massive landslide—nothing cinematic—but it was enough. Enough to tear across the narrow trail where they'd been about to step, enough to obliterate the path to the mule road, enough to send dust billowing into the air and leave a raw, jagged wound in the hillside.

Cassidy coughed, one arm over her face, jars clanking in the pack Lorenzo had taken from her. The dog barked furiously at the fallen earth as if she could intimidate it into rearranging itself.

They waited until the dust settled.

Lorenzo swore under his breath. "That's not good."

42

The path ahead was gone, buried under a fresh mound of loose rock and soil that still slid in small trickles.

"Can we cross it?" Cassidy asked.

"Not safely," Adriano said. He tested the edge with his boot; the earth crumbled away. "One wrong step and you ride it down the slope. It might not kill you, but it would hurt. A lot."

"Backtrack?" she said.

Lorenzo looked up toward the top of the damaged section. "We could try to climb higher and go around," he said slowly. "The slope is gentler up there. Probably. Maybe."

"So our choices are: break our legs, or gamble on your sense of 'probably,'" Cassidy said.

"You trust me," he said.

"I trust your cooking. This is different."

He squinted at the broken hillside, then frowned harder. "This isn't just erosion," he said. "Look." He pointed to the upper edge, where the soil had sheared away in a suspiciously clean line, exposing tree roots that had been cut.

Adriano followed his gaze. His face went cold. "Those roots didn't snap," he said. "They were severed."

Cassidy felt a chill despite the heat. "You're saying this was... helped?"

"Somebody weakened the slope," Lorenzo said. "Up top. Cut roots. Maybe dug a little. Waiting for the right rain or the right vibration to bring it down."

"Or the right people," Adriano added.

Cassidy stared at the rubble. "You think this was for us?"

"I think," he said, voice taut, "that Davide's people aren't the kind to give up after one botched spray job."

"Could also be unrelated," Lorenzo offered weakly. "Coincidences happen."

The dog whined.

"No," Cassidy said. "We don't get coincidences anymore."

Lorenzo sighed. "Fine. Sabotage. Happy?"

43

"No."

He surveyed the hill again. "We still need to get back before the heat really sets in," he said. "Higher path it is."

They climbed.

It was harder going—hands and knees in places, grabbing at scrub and rock to haul themselves upward, jars and packs clinking and shifting. The sun pressed down on the back of Cassidy's neck; sweat slicked her spine. Dirt worked its way under her nails. She tried not to think about the looseness of the soil beneath her boots.

At one point, a rock rolled under her foot; she slipped, heart lurching, but Adriano caught her wrist in a bruising grip and steadied her.

"You okay?" he asked.

"I hate this hill," she said through her teeth. "Tell it I hate it."

"It doesn't care," he said. "It just doesn't want you to die stupidly."

"Oh good," she muttered. "We have that in common."

Little by little, they edged around the damaged section and back onto firmer ground. From that vantage point, Cassidy could see the full pattern of the slide—where the cuts had been made, where the rocks had been loosened. Someone had come up here with tools and intention.

"They're trying to close exits," she said.

"Or corral us," Adriano said.

Lorenzo nodded grimly. "Let's not be corralled, then."

By the time they reached the mule road, Cassidy's legs trembled with fatigue. The asphodel jars clinked reassuringly in the pack.

"You know what I'd like right now?" she said.

"An apology from the universe?" Lorenzo suggested.

"Gelato," she said. "Lemon. Maybe pistachio. Something cold and sweet and absolutely free of moral complications."

"Yes," he said. "Gunshots and gelato. That seems to be the theme."

Cassidy almost smiled.

44

They made their way down the last incline, through another small stand of trees, and the vineyard finally came back into view —rows marching downhill, the farmhouse a stone anchor at the bottom.

From this distance, it looked like a postcard again.

Just a postcard where someone might be aiming back.

Messages and Missing Pieces

Silvia met them at the edge of the yard, shading her eyes. "You're late," she said. "I was about to start engraving your names on a memorial stone."

"We had a small disagreement with gravity," Cassidy said.

Enrico's dog trotted forward to greet her, tail wagging. Silvia scratched her ears. "Did you win?" she asked the dog.

The dog panted happily.

"She threw a rockslide at us," Lorenzo said. "We consider it a draw."

Enrico came out onto the porch, wiping his hands on a towel. He eyed the dirt, the scrapes, the sweat.

"You look like you got into a fight with a hill," he said.

"We did," Cassidy replied.

"Did you at least win against the flowers?" he asked.

Lorenzo held up the pack with a tired flourish. "We come bearing gifts."

Enrico's face lit. "Finally. Something good." Then it clouded again. "While you were gone, Giacomo called."

Cassidy's stomach clenched. "Is Nonna—"

"They're fine," Enrico said quickly. "Still alive. Still eating. Brunella has already tried to marry Giacomo off to three different women. He is traumatized."

Silvia snorted. "Good. Builds character."

45

"But," Enrico continued, "they had... visitors in the village. Strangers in a car asking questions about honey suppliers. Not at Brunella's house, but close enough that she saw them."

"Davide's men?" Adriano asked.

"Maybe," Enrico said. "Maybe not. Doesn't matter. Nonna says to tell you: 'Check the roots. Not all poison is in the honey.'"

Cassidy blinked. "Check the roots," she repeated.

"Like Marta," Lorenzo murmured. "With the slope."

"Not just honey," Cassidy said, hearing Marta's voice again. *He's not just touching honey. He starts with what's sweet and easy. Then he goes where the money is.*

"Oil," Adriano said. "Wine. Grain."

"People," Silvia added quietly.

Enrico nodded once. "You see why I don't like visitors."

They moved back into the kitchen, the antidote base jar still resting where they'd left it that morning. Lorenzo unpacked the asphodel carefully, laying the blooms out on the table. Enrico fetched a knife, a pot, and a smaller jar.

They worked again, this time with a new intensity. Slicing bulbs. Infusing them in warm liquid. Straining. Mixing the infusion into a small portion of the base. Stirring slowly, clockwise, following the instructions in the ledger exactly.

Cassidy read aloud, her mother's words steadying her. "Heat until it coats the spoon. Cool. Smell. Should be sweet with a bitter ghost."

"Very reassuring," Silvia muttered.

Adriano lifted the spoon when it was ready, letting a thick ribbon of antidote drip back into the jar. He inhaled carefully. "Sweet," he said. "But something underneath. Metallic, but less than before."

"That's the poison binder," Lorenzo said. "It's catching it. Holding it."

"We still have to know if it works," Cassidy said.

"Not on us," Silvia repeated.

46

"No," Lorenzo agreed. He reached for a second jar—the one he'd kept carefully to one side since Siena. It held honey that looked no different from any other: golden, viscous, innocent. It was anything but.

"We brought this from the warehouse in Modena," he said. "One of Davide's tainted batches. We know it makes people sick. If the antidote works, it should neutralize whatever he's put in here. At least partially."

Cassidy's stomach twisted. "So we mix them and... see what happens?"

"More or less," Lorenzo said.

"That's an incredibly stressful 'more or less,'" she said.

They set up like a science experiment—three small dishes, each labeled hastily by Silvia's sure hand.

DISH A: tainted honey alone.
DISH B: antidote alone.
DISH C: combination.

Lorenzo first warmed the tainted honey slightly until it loosened, then spooned equal amounts into A and C. He added a spoonful of antidote to B and to C, stirring the third dish until the two substances blended.

For a moment, nothing happened.

Then, very slowly, Dish C's contents thickened further, darkening slightly as if something inside was being pulled up and bound. Tiny bubbles rose to the surface—not the wild froth of a reaction gone wrong, but the slow, deliberate exhale of something shifting form.

Dish A—tainted honey alone—remained glossy and unchanged.

Cassidy leaned closer. "Is that... good?"

"It means something is happening," Lorenzo said. He touched a toothpick lightly to each dish, then held them under his nose in turn, inhaling carefully and spitting on the floor for good measure afterward.

"A," he said. "Metallic, wrong. Bitter at the end."

"B?"

"Sweeter. Still has bite, but it's… purposeful. Like a strong liquor."

"And C?"

He closed his eyes, sniffed again, and frowned in concentration.

"Less metal," he said. "The bitterness is there, but it's muted. Blunted. Something else has stepped in front of it."

"That sounds like an advertisement for a weird craft beer," Cassidy said.

"It sounds like it's binding some of the poison," Adriano said. "Not all. But some."

Lorenzo nodded reluctantly. "This is a first step," he said. "We don't know how strong the taint is in this sample. We don't know if one dose will be enough. But—" He tapped Dish C. "—this is doing something the honey on its own isn't doing."

"Which means," Cassidy said slowly, "we might actually be able to help people who have eaten this."

"In time," Adriano said. "If we can scale it. If we can get it into the right hands without it being destroyed."

"If," Silvia said grimly.

The room buzzed with too many thoughts.

Cassidy's gaze drifted back to the ledger. To the antidote page. Something about it had been tugging at her all afternoon, a faint itch at the back of her mind. Now she realized what it was.

There was a gap.

A section of the margin that had been trimmed too neatly. A faint line where a page might once have rested.

"Wait," she said.

The others looked at her.

She flipped back and forth quickly. The pages leading up to the antidote recipe were full—notes, sketches, cross-references. The one after it had a small, jagged remnant at the binding.

"She tore something out," Cassidy said, throat suddenly dry.

"Your mother?" Adriano asked.

48

"Or someone else." Cassidy traced the ragged edge with her thumbnail. "Something used to be here. Maybe a refinement. Maybe a second version. Maybe a distribution plan. Whatever it was, it was important enough that someone didn't want anyone else to see it."

Lorenzo swore under his breath.

"Who had access to this ledger besides you?" Silvia asked her.

"In Siena?" Cassidy thought quickly. "Me. Adriano. Lorenzo. Giacomo. Teresa. Pietro. Nonna. The woman from the Keepers."

"And before that?" Silvia pressed.

"I don't know," Cassidy said, frustration flaring. "My mother's people. The Keepers. Whoever she trusted enough to carry this around without losing it. I only know that when we saw it in the Siena cellar, that tear wasn't this obvious."

"Or you were too distracted by the whole 'your dead mother was in a secret food resistance' thing to notice," Lorenzo said gently.

"Valid," she conceded.

Silence settled again, heavier this time.

"So," Silvia said at last. "We have an antidote that maybe kind of partially works. A missing page that might have made it work better. A criminal who's expanding his poisoning empire beyond honey. And a hillside with booby-trapped roots."

"Also a terrifying shepherd woman on our side," Lorenzo added.

"True," Cassidy said. "Silver linings."

Adriano leaned over the ledger, staring at the torn edge as if he could will the missing information back onto the paper. "Whoever took that page is ahead of us," he said. "They know something we don't."

"Either they're trying to use the antidote themselves," Lorenzo said, "or they're trying to make sure no one can."

"Both options are bad," Silvia said.

Cassidy closed the ledger with more force than necessary. "Then we find them," she said. "Whoever it is. Whoever had their hands in this book after my mother. We find them, we get the missing piece, and we finish this."

"And if it's someone we thought we could trust?" Adriano asked quietly.

She met his gaze. "Then we stop them too."

Outside, the sun had started its slow slide toward the horizon, lengthening shadows across the vineyard. The day had been full—too full—but instead of feeling satisfied, Cassidy felt the ground shifting under her again.

A working prototype of an antidote.

A shepherd who threw rocks at wolves.

A missing page.

And somewhere, in the network of old allies and new enemies, a person holding a piece of the puzzle they desperately needed.

"We're a third of the way through this," she thought suddenly. Nine chapters. Three down. The story was pushing them forward whether they felt ready or not.

She looked up to find Adriano watching her, some unspoken question in his eyes. She didn't have an answer yet.

"Tomorrow," Lorenzo said. "We test more. We refine. We figure out who else has seen this ledger. And we start thinking not just about how to cure people…"

"…but how to keep them from needing a cure at all," Adriano finished.

"And," Enrico added from the doorway, arms crossed, "you eat. No one saves the world on an empty stomach."

His dog barked once in agreement.

Cassidy exhaled, squared her shoulders, and reached for her glass of water.

Tomorrow, they'd chase missing pages and deeper poison.

Tonight, they'd eat, breathe, and hold onto the fragile threads of hope they'd managed to weave on this chaotic hill in Montaione.

The story was just beginning to show its teeth.

Chapter 4 – The Sweet Front

Morning at Enrico's vineyard looked like a lie.

The sky was too blue. The hills were too gentle. The vineyard rows marched politely along the slope, leaves winking in the light as if they had no idea men with chemicals and guns had been here days ago. Enrico's rooster crowed late and indignant, offended by the very concept of time. Somewhere, a tractor coughed to life and Enrico swore at it through an open window.

Inside, the kitchen was already in controlled chaos.

Cassidy sat at the table with the ledger open in front of her, staring at the ragged edge where the missing page should have been. She'd been staring at it so long that the torn fibers had begun to blur and dance.

"Staring harder will not grow it back," Silvia said, sliding a plate of toast toward her.

"It might," Cassidy muttered. "We haven't ruled out spontaneous paper regeneration."

Adriano poured coffee, the dark liquid steaming as it hit the mug. "Magic is not our primary strategy," he said. "Unfortunately."

"Magic is never the primary strategy," Enrico said from the stove. "Magic is what you use when you have already ignored good advice and now you need a miracle."

"That feels like a personal attack," Cassidy said.

"If the shoe fits," he said.

Lorenzo came in from the yard, hair damp, phone in hand. "Giacomo says Nonna Vivi has challenged Brunella's neighbor to a bocce match," he reported. "He is worried for the neighbor's safety."

"Good," Silvia said. "Let her burn off steam there instead of here."

"Any more strange cars?" Adriano asked.

"Not near Brunella's," Lorenzo said. "But Giacomo heard talk in the village about new men asking questions about bulk honey deliveries. Same pattern. No names. Just... presence."

Cassidy rubbed her eyes. "They're feeling for weak spots," she said. "Testing how far they can push before someone pushes back."

"Then we push first," Adriano said.

"We can't push everywhere at once," Silvia pointed out. "We barely have an antidote that maybe works. We're three people, one dog, one enraged grandmother, and a small army of grumpy hill folk."

"Do not underestimate the hill folk," Enrico said, flipping something in a pan. "Or my dog. My Nina could run a small country if she wanted."

Nina wagged her tail under the table, as if to confirm.

Cassidy tapped the ledger. "We need information," she said. "Whoever tore this page out knows more than we do right now. The Keepers, my mother's network... somebody touched this book after she did."

"We should talk to Teresa again," Lorenzo said. "She knew more than she said in Siena."

"She also nearly got shot in Siena," Silvia replied. "She's probably not eager to pop back up on Davide's radar."

"So we don't drag her here," Cassidy said. "We go looking for traces instead. My mother was in Montaione at some point. She worked with Giulia. She met people, used suppliers, left footprints. If we walk the town, maybe we find where that missing page went before it vanished."

Adriano considered this. "A day in town won't fix everything," he said. "But we can't sit here and wait for someone else to move."

"And if Davide's fingers are already here," Lorenzo added, "we need to know how deep they go. Before we start dumping antidote into the system and hope for the best."

"What are you thinking?" Silvia asked.

He spread his hands. "Market. Pharmacy. Bar. Gelato shop. People talk. Merchants gossip. Especially about new suppliers with too much money."

"At last," Enrico said, turning from the stove with a pan of eggs, "someone suggests a plan that involves gelato."

Typical Italian Market Day

Montaione's medieval center perched on the hill above the vineyards like a stone crown. Narrow streets spiraled up to the main piazza, where the weekly market had spilled out in a riot of stalls and voices.

Cassidy inhaled as they entered the square. It smelled like everything at once: fresh basil, ripe tomatoes, cheese, flowers, sweat, coffee, soap, cigarettes. People moved through the crush with practiced ease, bags slung over shoulders, children dodging between legs like small, chaotic satellites.

"This is what you wanted," Adriano said quietly at her side. "When you first came here."

It was. This was the Italy from her daydreams. One with a view that launches a thousand dreams. Overripe and loud and alive. The Italy that existed in travel articles with titles like "Hidden Hilltop Towns You Must Visit Before You Die."

"Yeah," she said. "Back when I thought my biggest problem would be figuring out which cheese stall was the best."

"That one," Lorenzo said, pointing ahead without missing a beat.

She followed his finger. The cheese stall he indicated had a line three customers deep and a man behind the counter with arms like hams and a moustache that suggested a commitment to excellence.

"Of course you already know," she said.

He flashed a quick smile. "Some instincts are sacred."

They had split on the way into town: Adriano and Cassidy together; Lorenzo and Silvia promising to "blend in like normal

53

locals," which Cassidy translated as "acquire unnecessary snacks and eavesdrop shamelessly."

"I will stay near the car," Enrico had said. "I do not go near markets. Last time, a woman tried to sell me an antique door knocker. I have never recovered."

Now, in the crowded piazza, Adriano inclined his head toward a side street. "Pharmacy first," he said. "If anyone has noticed an uptick in mysterious symptoms, it will be the farmacia."

Cassidy nodded. "Then we walk the shops. Maybe look for anyone who reacts to the words 'honey' or 'Davide' with a suspicious twitch."

"And gelato," Lorenzo called as he and Silvia peeled off toward the far end of the square. "Information gathering requires sugar."

"Don't get shot," Cassidy said.

"We'll try," Silvia replied.

Symptoms Flaring Up

The pharmacy sat half a block off the main piazza—a narrow, tidy shop with a green cross sign and a bell on the door that jingled when they stepped inside. It smelled like disinfectant, talc, and faintly of dried herbs.

A woman in her fifties stood behind the counter, glasses perched on her nose, white coat neatly pressed. She looked up as Adriano and Cassidy entered, and her polite professional smile deepened with recognition when she saw Adriano.

"Buongiorno," she said. "Signor Vitale. It's been a while."

"Too long, Signora Rinaldi," he said. "Last thing I knew you were in Firenze. I didn't know that you transferred here. How's your husband?"

"Still insisting he's twenty-five," she said dryly. "His knee disagrees." Her gaze slid to Cassidy, lingering with curiosity but no judgment. "And this?"

"A friend," he said. "Cassidy."

"American," she observed.

"Yes," Cassidy said. "Sorry."

She chuckled. "We forgive you. Usually. What can I do for you two?"

Adriano rested his forearms casually on the counter. "Actually, we're looking for some information," he said. "Have you noticed any... unusual patterns lately? More people coming in with similar symptoms?"

Her brow furrowed. "You mean like flu?"

"Not exactly," Cassidy said carefully. "More like... fatigue. Nausea. Dizziness. Maybe heart flutters. Not quite food poisoning. Not quite anything obvious."

Rinaldi grew very still.

Adriano held her gaze. "You've seen something."

She hesitated. "I've seen... more complaints," she conceded. "People coming from the countryside mostly. Some from the next town. They say they feel off. Weak. Hearts racing. Some have trouble sleeping. Others are dizzy for no reason."

"How long?" Cassidy asked.

"A few months," Rinaldi said. "At first, I thought it was age. Stress. Heat. Then I realized some of the younger ones were saying the same things." She lowered her voice. "It feels systemic, not seasonal. As if something invisible has shifted."

"Anyone mention what they've eaten?" Adriano asked. "Any brand or product in common?"

"They all eat," she said dryly. "This is Italy. But..." She glanced toward the back room, then beckoned them closer. "If I say something, you didn't hear it from me."

"Of course," Adriano said.

"There's a new distributor," she said quietly. "For honey and sometimes other goods. I don't buy from him—I have my own suppliers—but enough shops in the area do. Cheap, pretty labels. Big promises about 'artisanal,' 'local,' 'pure.'" She snorted. "All words that mean nothing when printed by a man from the city."

Cassidy felt her pulse quicken. "You know his name?"

"I don't," she said. "He stays in the background. But his men drive vans with the same logo—sweet bee, golden drop, little Tuscan hill. Looks trustworthy to people who don't know better." She made a face. "Marketing."

Adriano slid a folded piece of paper from his pocket, the one they'd taken from a crate back in Modena. He opened it just enough for her to see the stylized bee stamped at the top.

Her mouth flattened. "Yes," she said. "That one."

"And you think there's a connection," he said.

"I think," she replied, "that ever since shops started selling more of that brand, I've seen more people come in asking why they feel like their bodies have betrayed them." She sighed. "But I have no proof. If I start accusing a company without evidence, I look like a hysteric. Or worse, I get sued."

Cassidy swallowed. "Has anyone... gotten worse?"

Rinaldi's gaze drifted toward the back again, as if she could see through walls. "One older man in the next village," she said softly. "A farmer. Strong. Never sick. He started feeling strange a few months ago. Thought it was age. Then he started forgetting words. His hands shook. His heart..." She pressed a hand to her own chest. "I sent him to the hospital in Florence last week. I haven't heard back."

"Do you have his name?" Cassidy asked.

She nodded, scribbled it down, slid the paper across the counter. "But if you go asking questions, do it quietly," she said. "Whoever is behind this, they don't like attention."

"We've noticed," Cassidy said.

Rinaldi studied her. "You're not from here," she said again. "But you're carrying yourself like someone who takes this personally."

"It is personal," Cassidy said. "For a lot of reasons."

The pharmacist nodded as if that made sense. "There's another thing," she added. "It might be nothing. But there's a gelato shop at the edge of the piazza—the new one with the shiny glass and the music too loud. They've started offering a 'Miele e Oro' flavor. Honey and something else. They brag about a special supplier. Say it's the same bee company. People love it. Lots of tourists. Lots of kids."

Cassidy's stomach dropped. "Honey gelato."

"Of course there is honey gelato," Rinaldi said. "This is not new. But this one..." She shook her head. "It makes me uneasy. Maybe I'm paranoid. Maybe I've worked in this town too long. But if I were looking for an easy way to put something inside a thousand bodies in one week..."

"...I'd give it away in little paper cups," Cassidy finished.

She and Adriano exchanged a loaded look.

"Thank you," he said to Rinaldi. "For trusting us."

"Don't make me regret it," she replied. "Bring me proof or bring me nothing. And if you get yourselves killed, do not bleed on my floor. I just had it mopped."

Gunshots and Gelato, Part One

At the far end of the piazza, in a corner that caught the afternoon light, the new gelato shop glittered.

It was painfully modern—sleek white counters, polished chrome, pastel signs with cursive fonts. Trendy music pulsed softly from inside. A group of teenagers clustered near the doorway, laughing with cones in their hands.

Above the door, a cheerful sign read: GELATO D'ORO. A smaller placard by the window advertised a new flavor in handwritten loops:

MIELE DORATO – honey from our special Tuscan bees! Taste the sunshine!

Lorenzo and Silvia stood across the street, half-hidden by a potted olive tree, pretending very badly to be uninterested.

"This is the worst stakeout I've ever seen," Cassidy said, coming up beside them.

"It's my first gelato stakeout," Silvia replied. "Be nice."

"Report?" Adriano asked.

"Flavor list inside," Lorenzo said. "Normal offerings—pistachio, hazelnut, stracciatella, dark chocolate. The honey one is new. Popular. People like the idea of 'local.'"

"They always do," Cassidy muttered.

"Guy behind the counter is local," Silvia said. "Young. Nervous. Keeps glancing at the door like he expects someone else to walk in."

"Who owns it?" Adriano asked.

"On paper? A company from Florence," Lorenzo said. "Real gelato people. They supply other shops too. But my friend at the bar says this place changed hands quietly a few months ago. New investors. New supply trucks. The ones with the bee logo."

"Of course," Cassidy said.

"And," Silvia added, "there has already been drama."

"Drama how?" Adriano asked.

She nodded toward the shop window. A small starburst crack marred the lower edge of the glass, spidering outward from a central point.

"Somebody threw a rock?" Cassidy guessed.

"Sure," Silvia said. "If rocks move that fast and come from that angle."

"Bullet," Adriano said flatly.

Lorenzo nodded. "Last week. Late at night. No one hurt. No police report filed, officially. But everyone nearby heard it. Bar owner says the next morning, two men in suits showed up to talk to the owner. Voices were… raised."

"So Davide's people are sending messages to their own shops now," Cassidy said. "Or someone else is trying to scare them."

"Either way, it confirms what Rinaldi said," Adriano replied. "The wolves are already here."

They watched as a family came out of the shop—two kids with honey-colored scoops in paper cups, parents chatting, utterly unaware that they might be eating evidence.

Cassidy's hands curled into fists. "We have to be able to test it," she said. "If we can prove that this flavor is tainted, that ties Davide's brand directly to people getting sick."

"And then what?" Silvia asked. "We stand in the piazza and shout that the gelato is trying to kill them? They'll think we're insane. Or that we're attacking a competitor."

"She's right," Lorenzo said. "Accusing people of poisoning their neighbors is… delicate."

"We don't accuse yet," Adriano said. "We collect samples. Quietly. Bring them back. Compare them to the honey we know is poisoned. See if the patterns match."

"And if they do?" Cassidy asked.

"Then we have leverage," he said. "Evidence. Something we can take to the Keepers. Or to someone who can blow this open in a way Davide can't bury easily."

"Like who?" Silvia asked. "The press?"

Cassidy thought of all the times she'd pitched stories and been told they were "too niche," "too complicated," "too damning to the wrong advertisers."

"Maybe," she said slowly. "But we'll need more than one scoop to convince anyone."

Lorenzo tilted his head. "So we buy gelato," he said. "Purely for research."

Silvia gave him a look. "You're enjoying this, aren't you?"

"No," he said. "Yes. Perhaps."

Cassidy exhaled. "Okay," she said. "Two samples of the honey gelato to go. One for the kitchen lab, one for a backup. No eating. No licking fingers. No taste tests. We treat it like a crime scene."

Lorenzo clutched his chest. "You wound me."

"We'll get you a non-murderous flavor after," she promised.

"And we watch for who's watching the shop," Adriano added. "If Davide's men are making regular stops, this is a node in his distribution network."

"And nodes can be cut," Silvia said.

They crossed the street.

Inside the Sweet Front

The air inside the gelato shop was cool and sweet. The full-display case glowed with rows of carefully swirled flavors, jeweled with toppings: pistachios, chocolate shavings, candied orange peel. The honey gelato sat front and center—a pale gold mound with a glossy sheen, drizzled artfully with a thin ribbon of amber honey.

The young man behind the counter straightened as they entered, smoothing his apron. His hair was carefully styled; his eyes carried dark shadows that didn't come from fashion.

"Buongiorno," he said. "What can I get for you?"

"Two small cups of the miel—" Cassidy began.

"Three," Lorenzo cut in. "We need more for accuracy."

"You're not eating it," she hissed.

He sighed dramatically. "Fine. Two."

"We'll take them to go," Adriano said.

The young man nodded, reaching for the scoop. "You're lucky," he said. "We almost ran out yesterday. It's been very popular."

"I can imagine," Cassidy said. "Where do you get the honey?"

He shot her a brief, wary look. "From a supplier," he said. "A new one. Very good quality. Very... premium."

Lorenzo leaned on the counter just enough to seem casual. "From around here?" he asked.

"From Tuscany," the man said. "That's what the paperwork says."

"Paperwork lies more than people," Silvia murmured.

The man's mouth twitched.

Cassidy studied him more closely. There was something in his posture—a stiffness, a way his eyes darted toward the door—that screamed: *I did not sign up for this level of tension when I chose a career in frozen desserts.*

"What's your name?" she asked.

He blinked. "Scusi?"

"Your name," she repeated. "So if this is the best gelato I've ever had, I know who to thank."

He hesitated, then gave in. "Marco."

"Nice to meet you, Marco," Cassidy said. "I'm Cassidy. This is Adriano, Lorenzo, Silvia. We're staying nearby."

He nodded, sliding lids onto the cups. "You should come back tonight," he said. "We stay open late when it's hot."

"Busy?" Lorenzo asked.

"Sometimes," Marco said. "Sometimes not. Depends on if the tourists feel like walking down this way."

Cassidy rested her forearms on the glass. "Looks like someone didn't want you open at all," she said, nodding toward the cracked window.

Marco's jaw tightened. "Kids," he said. "Drunk. With a pellet gun. They thought it would be funny."

"Nobody reported it," Adriano said mildly.

Marco's gaze snapped to him. "How do you know that?"

"I read the local paper," Adriano said. "They report when someone sneezes loudly. A gunshot, even a small one, would have made the front page."

Marco swallowed.

"It's not safe to have people like that around," Cassidy said gently. "Especially if they're connected to whoever's supplying your honey."

He stared at the honey bin as if it might start speaking. "I don't know anything about that," he said. "They told me to sell it. They

61

told me it would bring in customers. They told me not to ask questions."

"Who is 'they'?" Lorenzo asked.

Marco shook his head. "I don't know his name. I only ever see the same man. Cheap suit. Too much cologne. He comes in, checks the receipts, brings more honey and gelato base. Tells me I'm lucky to be part of a new brand. Says if I make trouble..." He trailed off.

Cassidy felt a chill. "Says what?"

"Just gives me a look," Marco said. "You know the kind. Like he's already seen your grave and he's thinking about the flower arrangements."

She chose her next words carefully. "Marco," she said, lowering her voice, "if the honey is making people sick—not definitely, but possibly—would you want to know?"

He stared at her, all the pretense draining away. Fear remained. And something like weary anger.

"I'm not stupid," he said. "I hear people. They talk in the piazza. 'Did you hear about so-and-so's son? He's been dizzy all summer.' 'Did you hear about old Signor Bartoli? In the hospital.' They say it's stress. Heat. Age." His hand tightened on the scoop. "My uncle collapsed last week. He works in a supermarket that sells that bee brand. He eats the samples, like everyone else."

"I'm sorry," she said.

Marco swallowed. "If there's something wrong with this, I don't want to be the one handing it to children," he said. "But if I stop selling it, they'll come back. And I..." He shook his head. "You should go. I've already said too much."

Adriano slid a card across the counter. It wasn't a business card —just a number and a name handwritten on the back of an old wine tasting flyer.

"If you decide you don't want to be in this alone," he said, "call this number. Ask for Giacomo. Tell him Marco from Montaione has a problem. He'll know what that means."

Marco stared at the card, then tucked it quickly into his apron pocket. "I didn't tell you anything," he said.

"No," Cassidy replied. "We figured it out all by ourselves."

He handed them the cups. "Be careful," he said. "They don't like people who ask questions."

"Fortunately," Cassidy said, "we're very bad at doing what people like."

Back at the Vineyard – Threads Tighten

The gelato samples rode back to the vineyard nestled in a portable cooler Enrico produced from somewhere, grumbling about "using good ice for bad purposes."

They set up their makeshift lab again in the kitchen, working with the focus of people who were very aware they were stirring something that might be trying to kill them.

Dish D: honey gelato alone.

Dish E: honey gelato plus antidote base.

Dish F: honey gelato plus tainted honey from the crate, to see if the profiles matched.

They melted small amounts, letting them liquefy, then stirred in corresponding components. The smell that rose from Dish D, once the cold had gone, was uncannily familiar.

"Same metallic hint," Lorenzo said. "Same bitter tail."

"And when we add the antidote," Adriano said, watching Dish E, "same reaction pattern as with the honey alone."

Cassidy felt part of her sink even as another part straightened with grim vindication. "So it's all connected," she said. "The jars in Modena. The honey in the countryside. The gelato in Montaione. All flowing through the same veins."

63

"Davide is building a brand," Silvia said. "Honey, gelato, who knows what else. He corrupts the sweetness. The name looks innocent so people don't question it."

"A nice metaphor," Enrico said tightly. "Evil hides in dessert."

"Not all dessert," Cassidy said. "Just… this one."

They tested the tainted gelato mixture with antidote. The same pattern emerged: thickening, bubbling, darkening slightly.

"It binds some of it," Lorenzo said. "But we still don't know if that's enough to reverse symptoms in a person."

"We need a real test," Silvia said reluctantly. "Someone who's been affected. Somewhere we can see the before and after."

Cassidy thought of the farmer Rinaldi had mentioned. The man in the hospital in Florence, hands trembling, words slipping away.

"If we could get a sample of his blood," she said slowly, "and compare it—"

"Hospital labs don't hand out patient samples like candy," Silvia said. "And walking into a medical facility waving a jar of homemade antidote is a good way to get committed."

"We can't do that yet," Adriano said. "We need more data. More tests. More missing pages."

At the mention of the missing page, the atmosphere shifted again.

Cassidy went back to the ledger, flipping through it. "We have to find out who took it," she said. "Someone who had access to this book between my mother and us. Someone still in the network. Or someone who betrayed it."

"How?" Lorenzo asked. "We don't even know everyone she worked with."

"No," she said. "But we know where she worked. The restaurant. The guesthouse. The village records. If she ever had to sign anything under her name or one of her aliases, the town will have a trace."

"Towns are good at keeping ghosts on paper," Adriano said.

"We already did one lap through Montaione today," Silvia said. "You want to go back?"

"Not right now," Cassidy said. "We're exhausted. We'll miss things. But soon. Tomorrow. We can divide tasks: someone at the archives, someone at the parish records, someone talking to old neighbors. People remember the woman who stirs things up."

"Especially if she looks like you," Lorenzo said.

Cassidy looked up sharply. "What do you mean?"

He regarded her for a moment. "You have her eyes," he said quietly. "Different color. Same way they look at a room like it owes them answers."

Something twisted in her chest. "You met her?"

"Once," he said. "Briefly. In Modena. She came through with my mom Giulia. They were arguing about vinegar and justice. It was... intense."

"You never thought to mention this before?" she asked, voice thin.

"It didn't seem... important," he said. "Back when I thought she was just a colleague. Then everything started happening at once and—" He spread his hands helplessly. "I forgot to tell you your mother terrified me for ten solid minutes."

Cassidy closed her eyes, picturing a woman like a storm cloud in a lab coat, arguing about viscosity and righteousness. It fit.

"Next time, mention it," she said roughly.

"I just did," he said.

Out of Nowhere

The first gunshot came in through the open window.

It snapped past Cassidy's ear and buried itself in the cabinet behind her with a vicious thud, splintering wood. She didn't even register the sound so much as the impact—a crack that jerked her out of her thoughts and into pure, cold instinct.

65

"Down!" Adriano shouted, already grabbing her shoulder and yanking her toward the floor.

The second shot shattered a jar on the counter—one of the empty ones, thank God—spraying glass and sticky residue across the tiles. Nina barked wildly, hackles up. Enrico swore in a creative combination of dialect and blasphemy.

Silvia dove behind the table, pulling the ledger with her. Lorenzo went low, rolling toward the window to slam it shut with one hand while the other shielded his face from the glass.

Three shots. Not a random burst. Controlled. Intentional.

Then silence.

Cassidy's heart slammed in her throat, breath coming too fast. She pressed one palm to the cool floor tiles, forcing herself to slow down, to listen.

No footsteps inside.

No door bursting open.

Just the echo of the shots fading over the hill and the distant, oblivious call of a bird.

"Everyone okay?" Adriano asked, voice tight.

Silvia checked herself, then the ledger. "Fine," she said. "Book's fine too."

"My jar," Enrico said mournfully.

"Your jar will be missed," Lorenzo said. He peered up cautiously toward the closed shutters. "Angle was wrong for someone in the yard. Shot came from higher up the hill."

"A warning," Adriano said. "If they wanted to hit us, they would have aimed differently."

"They aimed at my cabinet," Enrico snapped. "It held my favorite pan."

"Message received," Cassidy said, swallowing. "They know we're here. They know we're working. And they want us to know they know."

"In this country, you send a cake to say hello," Enrico muttered. "Not bullets."

Adriano helped Cassidy sit up, his hand lingering on her shoulder. "You're sure you're not hurt?" he asked.

"I'm fine," she said. Her voice shook anyway. "Mostly annoyed."

"That's healthy," Silvia said. "Channelling fear into anger. Very productive."

Lorenzo got to his feet carefully, keeping his body angled away from the window as he eased the shutter open just enough to look out.

"What do you see?" Silvia asked.

"Nothing now," he said. "Just the slope." He squinted. "Maybe... there. A glint. On the ridge. Someone retreating toward the treeline."

"Can you tell who?" Adriano asked.

"No," Lorenzo said. "But I'd bet my best knife it's the same wolves Marta chased off her hill."

Cassidy stood, legs unsteady, and moved to join him. From this angle, the ridge looked innocent. Too innocent. A smear of rocks. A stand of trees. The sun glancing off something metallic before it disappeared.

"Do you think they followed us from town?" she asked.

"Or they were already watching," Adriano said. "Waiting for confirmation we'd found what we needed from the hills."

"And now they know we have the asphodel, the partial antidote, and a working theory on how their gelato is killing people," Silvia said grimly. "They're escalating."

"They're scared," Lorenzo said.

"Scared men with guns are worse than calm ones," Enrico pointed out.

Cassidy rubbed the bridge of her nose. "Okay," she said. "So. In the last twenty-four hours, we've met a shepherd who throws rocks at criminals, nearly been taken out by a sabotage rockslide, discovered honey gelato is part of the poisoning network, and been shot at in a kitchen."

"It's been a busy day," Lorenzo said.

"Yesterday was also a busy day," she said.

"We're on a roll," he said.

She laughed, a short, sharp sound that surprised her. "I don't know if we're winning or just making them more creative," she said.

"Both," Adriano said. "We're forcing them to react. That means they're not fully in control."

Silence fell again, this time electric rather than empty. The three dishes on the counter—D, E, F—sat undisturbed amid the shattered glass, little pools of evidence.

Cassidy crossed the room and carefully moved them away from the broken cabinet. "We can't stop now," she said quietly. "Not when we're finally seeing the shape of this thing."

Silvia nodded. "We don't stop," she said. "We shift. We get smarter. We assume someone is watching every move."

"Which means," Lorenzo said, "we cannot keep the ledger in the obvious place."

Enrico bristled. "My kitchen is not obvious."

"Your kitchen has just been upgraded to target," Lorenzo replied. "Welcome to the club."

They ended up hiding the ledger in the most unglamorous place possible: inside a flour sack in the pantry, wrapped in waxed cloth, buried beneath regular, innocent flour.

"No one ever checks the flour," Enrico said with satisfaction. "Except me. And I will forget it's there by tomorrow."

"That's not comforting," Cassidy said.

"It is for your enemies," he replied.

Emerging Patterns

The rest of the afternoon unspooled in fits and starts—cleaning up glass, sending a coded message back to Giacomo about the shots ("The hill has teeth"), brewing more coffee, sketching out a map of

Davide's likely network: honey, gelato, supermarket chains, export lines.

Cassidy sat at the table with a pen and a sheet of paper, drawing circles and arrows: Modena warehouse, Siena tunnels, Florence distributors, Montaione gelato, rural pharmacies. The lines between them multiplied, intersected.

"It's like a spiderweb," she said. "We tug one thread, something moves three towns over."

"We need a bigger tug," Silvia said.

"We need the missing page," Adriano said. "I keep coming back to that. Your mother knew this might happen. She left you enough to get started, but the details—the scaling, the way to insert the antidote into the supply chain without setting off alarms—that's probably what she wrote on the page she tore out."

"Or someone else tore out," Cassidy said.

"Either way," he said, "someone out there has the blueprint. We're building from half a recipe."

"Wouldn't be the first time," Enrico muttered. "My cousin's aunt cooked like that for fifty years."

"The difference is," Lorenzo said, "if we get this wrong, people die."

"So we find the person with the page," Silvia said. "Where do we look first?"

Cassidy stared at the map. Her eyes landed on Florence. Then Siena. Then back.

"The Keepers," she said. "My mother's group. They're the ones who'd care enough to preserve it. Or hide it. Or use it. Teresa might not know where it is. But someone in that network does."

"And you think they'll just tell us," Silvia said.

"No," Cassidy said. "But they might tell the right story to the right person if we ask the right question. Or they might slip up. Or..." She inhaled sharply as an idea hit. "Or they might have been trying to reach us already."

She dug in her bag and pulled out her phone, scrolling through messages. One in particular—the strange one she'd gotten two days ago, before Siena blew up—suddenly looked different in hindsight.

A number she didn't know. A single line: *Not all pages belong in books. Some belong in mouths.*

She'd dismissed it then as spam or spam-adjacent poetry.

"Look at this," she said, turning the screen toward the others.

Lorenzo squinted. "Creepy," he said. "And vague."

"Exactly like the Keepers," Adriano said.

"It came in the day before we found out about the missing page," she said. "It might not be connected. But if it is…"

"Someone is telling you the antidote doesn't just live on paper," Silvia said. "It lives in recipes. In chefs. In people."

"Giulia," Lorenzo said slowly. "And your mother. And maybe others. If they didn't trust the ledger to survive, they could have hidden the key inside someone's head."

"So the missing page might not be the only copy," Cassidy said. "It might just be a backup. The real 'page' might be in somebody's hands. Or in a recipe that looks innocent until you tweak one ratio."

"Which means," Adriano said, leaning forward, "we might not need the paper as much as we thought. We need the person. Or the dish."

Cassidy's mind raced. "If my mother did that, she'd have left some kind of trail," she said. "A dish she always made a certain way. A recipe she guarded. A note in the margins of something that looks unrelated."

"Where did she work most often?" Silvia asked.

"Mostly with Giulia," Cassidy said. "In Modena. In pop-up dinners. Private events." She frowned. "There was also… a supper in Florence she mentioned once in an email. Something about 'feeding the future.' I thought she was being poetic."

"Feeding the future sounds like a Keepers meeting," Lorenzo said.

"And if they served something special there," Adriano added, "it might be the key. The antidote in edible form."

"Which would explain why Davide is so focused on honey and gelato," Silvia said. "If the Keepers tried to fight him via dessert, he'd respond in kind."

Cassidy rubbed her temples. "So now, on top of everything else, we're looking for a lost dinner party," she said. "Great."

"Better than a lost page," Lorenzo said. "At least you can ask people what they ate."

"Assuming they remember," she said.

"In Italy," Enrico said, "people always remember what they ate."

The Night Before Everything Tilts

The sun bled slowly out of the sky, leaving behind a pink wash that stained the clouds. The vineyard sank into shadow, the neat rows dissolving into darker bands across the hills. Lights came on one by one in the farmhouse, the guesthouse, the neighboring properties that had seen more seasons than any of them would.

Dinner was simple that night by Enrico standards—grilled vegetables, leftover pasta crisped in a pan until the edges caramelized, a salad scattered with torn basil and shavings of pecorino. No heavy wine. No limoncello. Just water and one modest carafe of red "for morale," as Lorenzo put it.

They ate around the table, the day's events settling over them like dust.

"Tomorrow," Cassidy said, "we go to the archives. Parish, municipal, whatever we can access. We look for my mother's name, her aliases, her signature. We see where she officially intersected with this town. Maybe that leads us to who tore the page. Or who attended the Florence supper."

"I'll go with you," Adriano said.

71

"I'll talk to the bar owner again," Lorenzo said. "See what else he's heard from the trucks. Maybe I can get a copy of a delivery slip. Something that ties Davide's company to the gelato chain more directly."

"I'll stay here," Silvia said. "Guard the antidote. Answer messages from Giacomo. Try not to get shot in the kitchen again."

"I will be everywhere," Enrico said. "Yelling."

"That's your best role," Lorenzo said.

Cassidy watched them, the easy way their banter wrapped around harder truths. It felt like standing in the eye of a storm — momentary stillness, knowing the winds would pick up again soon.

After dinner, she stepped outside alone for a while, standing at the edge of the yard where the dirt path met the first vine row. The air had cooled. The sky had gone full indigo, one star already pricking the surface.

From somewhere up the slope, an owl called. The same ridge where the earlier shots had come from was now just a shadow against the sky.

She hugged her arms around herself.

Footsteps approached behind her, soft in the dirt.

"You keep coming out here," Adriano said quietly.

"It keeps trying to kill us," she replied. "I feel like we should at least keep each other updated."

He came to stand beside her, hands in his pockets, gaze moving over the darkened rows. For a moment, they just breathed together.

"You did well today," he said.

She snorted. "We got shot at again."

"We found proof," he said. "Gelato. Network. Something we can use. And we're not dead yet. That counts as well."

"Your metrics are wild," she said.

He turned slightly, studying her profile. "You're scared," he said. It wasn't a question.

"Yes," she said. "I am. I'm also angry. And tired. And weirdly hungry again."

"We can fix two of those things," he said. "Maybe three."

She laughed softly. "Which two?"

"Food and tired," he said. "Angry we keep. Scared we... work with."

She nodded. "Tomorrow might be worse," she said.

"Yes," he said honestly. "But it might also be better. That's the thing about doing something." He shrugged. "You create room for better."

She turned to face him fully, the faint porch light catching the edges of his features. "When this is over," she said, "if it ever ends, and we get to have that boring life with coffee and arguing about dessert... do you think it will feel real? Or will we always be waiting for the next gunshot?"

He didn't answer right away. When he did, his voice was steady.

"I think," he said, "that if we survive this, we'll have earned every boring argument a thousand times over. And if the world still tries to shoot at us, at least we'll have better locks. And maybe a dog army."

"Nina would like that," she said.

"Nina would be general," he replied.

They stood there until the night grew deeper and the chill started to bite. Then they went inside.

Later, lying in the dark with his arm around her again, Cassidy stared at the ceiling and listened to the quiet creaks of the house, the distant hum of a car on the lower road, the faint rustle of leaves.

Somewhere out there, men in cheap suits were drawing new lines on their own maps. Davide was making moves they couldn't see yet. The missing page was in someone's hands. A gelato shop was scooping poison into paper cups under fluorescent lights.

Tomorrow, they'd go into town to dig through dusty records and living memories, trying to find the thread her mother had left hidden in the everyday.

Tomorrow, the story would tilt again. She could feel it.

73

For now, she let her eyes close, anchoring herself in the warmth beside her and the knowledge that, just for the moment, the hill was quiet.

The sweetness, she thought, might yet have something to say.

Chapter 5 – Paper Ghosts and Poisoned Promises

Cassidy woke to the sound of a printer jamming three rooms away. For a second, still halfway in a dream where her mother scribbled recipes on the sky, she thought she was back in an office somewhere—flourescent lights, stale coffee, deadlines. Then the rooster crowed off-key, a tractor backfired, and Enrico shouted something about "THIS STUPID MACHINE" in a mixture of Italian and profanity she was pretty sure wasn't in any official phrasebook.

Reality reassembled itself: Montaione. Vineyard. Poisoned honey. Missing page. Gunshots through the kitchen window.

And today: records.

She rolled over. Adriano was already sitting on the edge of the bed, buttoning his shirt, the early light from the window drawing clean lines along his shoulders. He glanced back when she moved, something soft flickering across his face.

"Buongiorno," he said.

"Is Enrico having a fight with office equipment?" she croaked.

"Yes," Adriano said. "The municipality sent him something to print and sign. He believes printers are a government conspiracy."

"He's not wrong," she muttered.

He smiled, then sobered. "You don't have to come today," he said. "To the archives. I can go with Lorenzo."

She frowned. "That's adorable, but no."

"Cassidy—"

"This is about my mother," she said. "My ledger. My almost-ghost. Besides, if you leave me here and someone shoots at the house again, I will be very annoyed to die in my pajamas."

He sighed. "You are infuriating."

"Thank you."

Downstairs, the kitchen smelled like toast and barely-suppressed rage. Enrico glared at a battered desktop printer perched on a side table as if it owed him money. The machine whirred reluctantly.

"It works better if you don't shout," Silvia said, stirring sugar into her coffee.

"It understands fear," Enrico replied. "Fear is good for electronics."

Lorenzo sat at the table with his phone and a notebook, scrolling and scribbling in alternating bursts. He looked up as Cassidy entered.

"City archivist opens at nine," he said. "Parish office is open from ten to twelve if the priest feels like it. Bar owner is available 'whenever my wife stops telling me to fix the tap.'"

"Very precise," Cassidy said, pouring herself coffee.

"Welcome to small-town scheduling," he said.

"Any more messages from Giacomo?" Adriano asked.

Silvia shook her head. "Last one was last night. 'Nonna has won bocce. Neighbors are afraid. Nina stole a sausage. Situation stable.'"

"Good," Cassidy said. "One less thing to panic about."

They ate quickly—toast, jam, coffee, a slice of leftover frittata Enrico insisted would "protect the brain from bureaucracy." Outside, the hills glowed with that bright, optimistic morning light that felt personally offensive given the circumstances.

"Schedule," Silvia said, tapping her mug like a gavel. "Team Records: Cassidy and Adriano. Town archives, parish offices, anyone who's ever stacked paper near your mother. Team Gossip: Lorenzo. Bars, market, any place where people complain about supply chains. Team Defensive: me and Nina. We stay here, guard the antidote, try not to get shot at again."

"And you call us if anything happens," Adriano said.

She raised an eyebrow. "Obviously. I enjoy screaming into telephones."

Lorenzo slid his notebook into a satchel. "I'll also swing by the bar where the drivers drink," he said. "See if any of Davide's

76

distribution guys have a habit of running their mouths after a few grappe."

"Be careful," Cassidy said. "Men who move poison for a living aren't known for their discretion, but they're very good at holding grudges."

"I'm charming," Lorenzo said. "I'll be fine."

"That's what they put on so many tombstones," she replied.

He grinned. "If I die, you can write it in a very moving way."

She tried not to think about how often they joked like that now.

Enrico's Nina trotted to the door as they left, tail wagging anxiously. Enrico pointed a stern finger at her. "You stay," he said. "Guard house. Bark at postman."

Nina huffed, then padded back to her spot under the table, clearly offended but loyal.

Adriano's car—a sturdy, anonymous hatchback that looked like it had survived several bad decisions already—waited in the driveway. As they climbed in, Cassidy glanced once more up the hill, toward the ridge where yesterday's shots had come from.

Nothing moved. Just trees. Rocks. Sky.

She buckled her seatbelt anyway.

The Archivist and the Ghost

Montaione's municipal building was a squat, dignified structure on the edge of the old center, with flaking pale-yellow paint and a doorway that had seen several generations of disgruntled taxpayers. A handwritten sign announced: *ARCHIVIO STORICO – SUONARE IL CAMPANELLO.*

Cassidy rang the bell.

A voice shouted, "ARRIVO!" from somewhere deep within, followed by the sound of footsteps, then something metallic falling over.

"Confidence-inspiring," she murmured.

The door opened to reveal a woman in her sixties, hair piled into a loose gray knot, reading glasses dangling from a chain. She wore a cardigan the color of moss and an expression that said: if you're here about parking tickets, turn around.

"Yes?" she said.

"Buongiorno, Signora," Adriano said smoothly. "We were hoping to consult some old records. If you have a moment."

She squinted at him, then at Cassidy. "What kind of records?"

"Event permits, business licenses, residency registrations," Cassidy said. "From about... ten to fifteen years ago. We're... doing some research." She flashed what she hoped passed for a professional, non-threatening smile. "I'm a journalist."

The woman's eyebrows lifted a fraction. "American?"

"Yes. Sorry."

A pause. Then a faint, amused exhale. "I'm Anna," she said. "Archivist. Official guardian of dust and bad handwriting. Come in, but don't expect miracles. This is not Florence."

"Miracles are overrated," Cassidy said.

Anna led them down a corridor that smelled like old paper and lemon cleaner. The archive room itself was larger than Cassidy expected—walls lined with metal shelves, file boxes stacked neatly, a long table in the center under a humming fluorescent tube.

"This is... beautiful," Cassidy said before she could stop herself.

Anna gave her a look usually reserved for people who enjoyed watching paint dry. "You are the first person to say that," she said. "Ever."

"I mean, functionally beautiful," Cassidy amended. "Narratively. All these lives in these boxes."

"That I believe," Anna said. "What exactly are you looking for?"

Cassidy glanced at Adriano. They'd rehearsed this.

"I'm trying to trace work my mother did," she said. "She was here, in Montaione, years ago. We think she might have registered

78

something—a cooking workshop, a dinner, a rental. But she used different names. We have a few to try."

She handed over a small list they'd made at breakfast: her mother's real name, plus the pseudonyms Cassidy had found in old emails and notes—Catherine Moretti, C. M. Ellis, Cat Morandi.

Anna scanned it, her expression tightening just slightly. "I remember this one," she said, tapping Catherine Moretti. "Tall woman. Serious eyes. Very specific questions about where she could host 'small gatherings' without attracting attention."

Cassidy's heart thudded. "She was here?"

"Twice," Anna said. "Maybe three times. Hard to forget." She walked toward a set of shelves. "Event permits from that period are here. Let's see if the state hasn't eaten them."

They spent the next hour in a haze of paper.

Anna pulled out boxes, stacked them on the table. Cassidy and Adriano leafed through file folders, scanning permit forms, rental agreements, photocopied ID cards. The forms were mind-numbingly similar—birthday parties, wine tastings, food tours.

Then Cassidy saw it.

Her mother's handwriting, careful and slightly slanted, filling out a field labeled: *DESCRIZIONE DELL'EVENTO*.

She read aloud under her breath. "Private culinary workshop. Limited guests. Focus on honey, oil, and preservation of traditional methods."

The name at the top: *Catherine Moretti*. The contact number was one Cassidy recognized from an old phone bill she'd once found in a box of her mother's things.

The venue: *Sala Comunale – Piano Superiore*, the community hall above the archives.

Anna peered over Cassidy's shoulder. "Ah, yes," she said. "That one."

"You remember?" Cassidy asked, voice tight.

"She insisted the windows could not face the street," Anna said. "Said it made people self-conscious. She brought her own honey in unmarked jars. The whole room smelled like a beekeeper's nightmare for three days afterward." Anna tapped a line near the bottom. "She also paid in cash and refused the municipal coffee. That's how you know a person has secrets—they don't trust public coffee."

Cassidy's throat constricted. "Do you remember anything else?"

Anna squinted at the form. "There was a second permit," she said. "She came back some months later with another woman. Dark hair. Sharp. Beautiful like a knife you're afraid to touch."

"Giulia," Adriano said hoarsely.

Anna moved to another box, flipping through. "Yes. Here." She pulled out a thinner file and laid it on the table.

This time, the description read: *Cena Privata – Solo Invito. Tema: "La Notte del Miele"*.

Private dinner. Invitation only. Theme: The Night of Honey.

The names listed as organizers: *Catherine Moretti & Giulia Bianchi.*

Venue: *Convento di Santa Lucia – Sala Refettorio.*

"A convent," Cassidy said. "Of course it's a convent."

"Abandoned one," Anna said. "Up the road, ten kilometers. Belonged to the diocese. They rented out the refectory for weddings and retreats before they sold it to some investors."

Cassidy scanned the rest of the form. "Do you know what this dinner was for?" she asked.

"I didn't ask," Anna said. "But I remember the guests. Not their names, but the... atmosphere. People who walked like they were used to edges. One old man kissed my hand and thanked me for 'protecting the paper.' It was odd."

"Keepers," Adriano murmured.

Cassidy's fingers shook slightly as she flipped the form over. In one margin, barely visible, someone had scribbled a note: *menu finalized with E.V.* The initials were underlined twice.

"E.V.," she said. "Does that mean anything to you?"

80

Anna frowned. "Could be anyone. Elena, Elisa, Eva, Enrico if he was drunk and trying to be mysterious. But there is one..." She tapped her lip. "Elena Valenti. She was in charge of catering for some church events. Very involved in food collectives. She helped organize farmer markets, too. She signed some permits around that time."

She went to another drawer, rifled in a separate folder, and pulled out a business card yellowed at the edges: *Elena Valenti – Cucina Etica, Firenze & Toscana.*

A logo—a simple line drawing of a spoon and a bee—sat next to the name.

Cassidy's heart gave a weird little jolt. "Cucina Etica," she read. "Ethical Kitchen."

"Very lofty name," Anna said. "She worked with co-ops, small producers, people who liked to talk about justice while eating cheese. Haven't seen her in years. Maybe she found a less exhausting job."

Cassidy turned the card over. An address in Florence, near the Oltrarno. A phone number that might or might not still work.

"Elena was involved with the dinner," Adriano said. "If the missing page is about scaling the antidote, and they tested an edible version at 'La Notte del Miele,' she would know how it was served. How it was hidden."

"And if someone tore that page out of the ledger and gave it to a living person instead..." Cassidy said, "she might be that person."

"Or she knows who is," Adriano added.

Cassidy looked at Anna. "Do you remember anything else about the dinner?" she asked. "Anyone else who stood out?"

The archivist considered. "The kitchen smelled like citrus and thyme," she said slowly. "One man had hands like a butcher and eyes like a priest. Another woman wore a bee brooch and kept counting people as they left. Your mother..." She shook her head "Your mother looked tired. Not physically. Like someone who'd been in a long argument with a wall."

81

Cassidy swallowed around the lump in her throat. "That sounds right."

Anna softened. "She came in once, after the permits," she said. "To thank me. Said the town had been kinder to her than some cities." She squeezed Cassidy's shoulder gently. "She didn't say she had a daughter."

"She didn't... talk about me much," Cassidy said. It came out more brittle than she meant it to.

"Maybe she was keeping you safe," Anna said. "Or maybe she was stubborn and foolish. Both are common diseases in mothers."

Cassidy let out a breath that was almost a laugh. "Accurate."

Adriano laid a hand on the table near hers, not quite touching, steadying. "We're grateful," he said to Anna. "This helps more than you know."

Anna nodded. "Bring the forms back," she said. "I'll pretend I didn't see you photocopy them."

"You're very kind," Cassidy said.

"I'm old," Anna replied. "I have decided which rules are stupid."

Parish Stories and Quiet Warnings

The parish office was a small annex attached to a modest church, its door propped open with a stone. Inside, the smell of wax and paper mingled with dust filtered through stained glass. A calendar of saints hung slightly askew above a filing cabinet.

The priest was younger than Cassidy expected—late thirties, maybe, with kind eyes and the faint outline of a tattoo peeking from under his collar when he moved his arm. His name, according to the little plaque on his desk, was **Don Paolo**.

"How can I help you?" he asked, when they explained they were looking into past events connected to the Convento di Santa Lucia.

82

"We heard the diocese used to rent out the refectory," Adriano said. "For dinners, retreats. There was one in particular—La Notte del Miele."

Don Paolo's eyes flickered. Just once. But Cassidy saw it.

"I was still in seminary then," he said slowly. "But I heard about it. It wasn't a parish event."

"What kind of event was it?" Cassidy asked.

He hesitated, then gestured to the chairs. "Sit," he said. "Otherwise my neck will hurt from looking up at you."

They sat.

"For the record," he said, "the Church likes to know what happens on its property. At least on paper. That dinner... was presented as a private gathering for food producers and activists. Ethical sourcing, environmental stewardship, that sort of thing. Good causes." He folded his hands. "But there was something... more. My predecessor mentioned it once. Said they were 'fighting a different kind of sin.'"

"How so?" Adriano asked.

"He didn't explain," Don Paolo said. "But he was... worried. Not about the people. About the consequences. He said, 'When you tell a man his food is killing him, he might thank you. Or he might decide to kill you first.'"

"That sounds about right," Cassidy muttered.

"Do you know who organized it?" Adriano pressed.

"The permits were filed by the town," Don Paolo said. "But the key was picked up by a woman from Florence. Dark hair. Bee brooch. Talked very fast."

"Bee brooch," Cassidy repeated. "Anna mentioned her too."

"She gave a donation to the church," he added. "For the use of the space. A generous one, for a group that claimed to be 'informal' and 'grassroots.' That made me suspicious." He smiled faintly. "I was young. Now I'm just suspicious on principle."

"Do you still have any record of her name?" Cassidy asked.

He opened a drawer, rifled through a tidy stack of envelopes, then pulled out an old receipt book. "We keep records," he said. "God likes receipts."

He flipped through pages until he found one, then turned it toward them.

DONAZIONE – CENA "NOTTE DEL MIELE" – ELENA VALENTI, PER CONTO DI "CIRCOLO CUCINA ETICA".

Elena again. Front and center.

"She gave in her own name," Cassidy said.

"Which either means she was honest," Adriano said, "or she was very confident no one would ever ask questions."

"Do you know what happened to the convent?" Cassidy asked the priest. "Anna said it was sold."

He nodded. "Some investors from Florence turned it into a 'spiritual retreat center' for a few years. Yoga, meditation, wine tastings marketed as 'mindful.'" He made a face. "Then they ran out of money. Or patience. It's been half-used ever since. A few events. A few weddings. Nothing consistent."

"Could someone still be using it now?" Adriano asked.

"It's possible," he said. "The current owner lives abroad, I'm told. Leaves a local agent to manage bookings."

"Do you know who?" Cassidy asked.

He hesitated. "Cassidy," he said, and her name sounded strange and gentle in his accent, "you are not asking these questions for a story, are you?"

She met his gaze. "I'm asking them so people don't die."

He nodded slowly, as if he'd expected that answer and still hoped to be wrong. "There's a woman who handles the convent now," he said. "Goes by Signora Fabbri. She also has connections with catering companies. Helps coordinate local suppliers for big events. If someone wanted to use that space quietly, she would know."

84

"Thank you," Adriano said.

Don Paolo sighed. "I didn't tell you any of this," he said. "Officially, I care only about souls. Unofficially..." He shrugged. "I don't like the feeling in the air lately. People come to confession talking about fatigue, fear, not knowing why their bodies feel wrong. Something is... off. If you are trying to set it right, I'm not going to stop you."

Cassidy's throat tightened. "We're trying," she said.

He gave her a small, sympathetic smile. "Then may you be annoying to all the right people," he said. "And may they be too stupid to see you coming."

Bar Talk and Delivery Routes

While Cassidy and Adriano swam through paper and parish memory, Lorenzo swam through espresso and gossip.

The bar on the corner of the piazza was the kind of place that accumulated men in the late morning—the ones who claimed to be "between jobs" but somehow always had time for coffee and arguments about soccer. Lorenzo slid in among them with the ease of someone who considered bars a second living room.

"Caffè macchiato," he told the barman. "And whatever pastry looks least like a crime."

The barman, a thickset man with a permanent frown named Mario, grunted and slapped a small cup on the counter. "You look too awake," he said. "It's suspicious."

"I had a good breakfast," Lorenzo replied. "Our host cooks like he's trying to keep us from running away."

Mario snorted. "Enrico? He cooks like he's punishing you for existing."

"Same result," Lorenzo said.

He nodded toward the cluster of men at the neighboring tables. "Busy today."

"Always busy when there's talk," Mario said.

"Talk about what?" Lorenzo asked innocently.

Mario rolled his eyes. "Trucks. Always trucks lately. New ones, from the south. From the city. From companies no one knows, but somehow they have contracts with every supermarket in a fifty-kilometer radius. People like what they sell because it's cheap. Of course they do. People never remember cheap comes with hidden tax."

"What kind of goods?" Lorenzo asked, carefully casual. "Honey? Oil? Pasta?"

"All of it," Mario said. "And there's talk of a big event next week. Two nights from now." He wiped a glass. "Promotion. Live music. Free samples."

"Free samples of what?" Lorenzo said, though he could taste the answer already.

"Honey," Mario said. "And gelato. They're calling it 'La Notte del Dolce.' They'll set up stalls in the piazza, bring in chefs, influencers, whatever that means." He grimaced. "The new gelato shop is involved, of course. The one with the cracked window."

"Of course," Lorenzo murmured. "Do you know who's organizing it?"

"On the posters, it's the comune," Mario said. "But someone else is paying. Someone with money. You think the town has budget for fireworks? Please."

One of the men at the nearest table—thin, with a nicotine-stained moustache—leaned in. "My cousin drives for them," he said. "The bee trucks."

"The same cousin who crashed into a ditch last year?" Mario said. "I don't trust his opinion of roads, let alone employers."

The man waved him off. "He says they're expanding," he insisted. "New routes. New products. They're even talking about vitamin-fortified honey drinks for kids. 'Energia naturale.'" He chuckled darkly. "Anything to make a euro."

Lorenzo's skin crawled.

Another man, older, set down his paper. "And what about all these people feeling sick?" he asked. "My neighbor can't walk up the stairs without his heart racing. Doctor says his tests are fine. He wasn't like this before."

"Old age," someone muttered.

"He's younger than you."

"Then it's the heat."

"It's October."

They argued in a circle, chasing their own tails.

Lorenzo took a sip of his coffee, then said, just loud enough, "Sometimes it's not age or heat. Sometimes it's what we put in our mouths."

The table went quiet.

"Food is food," moustache-man said after a moment. "We've always eaten. We're still here."

"We didn't always have men from god-knows-where bringing us products with pretty labels and no history," Lorenzo said calmly. "When you stop knowing where your food comes from, you stop knowing what's in it."

Mario grunted approval. "Finally, someone says something intelligent."

The older man frowned. "You saying the bee trucks are bad?"

"I'm saying," Lorenzo replied, "that when someone offers you a lot of sweetness for very little money, you should be suspicious. Real sweetness costs."

"This is why I don't eat dessert," Mario said.

"You don't eat dessert because your wife hides the sugar," moustache-man said.

They laughed, the tension easing slightly. But the ideas had been planted. Lorenzo could see it in their faces—the doubt, the glances, the mental tallying of what they'd eaten, what they'd bought.

As he left, Mario leaned across the counter. "Be careful how you talk," he said quietly. "Some people don't like questions."

"Good thing I'm not here to be liked," Lorenzo said, sliding a few coins onto the saucer.

"Then you'll do well," Mario replied.

Outside, Lorenzo paused at the bulletin board plastered with flyers—language classes, apartments, lost cats. A new poster had gone up overnight: a bright, cheerful design with a cartoon bee, music notes, and a gelato cone.

LA NOTTE DEL DOLCE – 2 GIORNI DI MUSICA, GELATO, E DOLCI A BASE DI MIELE.

Sponsored by: *DolceVero* (the bee logo) + Comune di Montaione + Local Partners.

He snapped a photo and sent it to Cassidy with a single line: *We have a ticking time bomb in the piazza.*

Crossed Wires

Back at the vineyard, Silvia was washing dishes she'd already washed once. When she was stressed, she either cleaned or threatened violence. Today, the plates were lucky.

Her phone vibrated on the counter. She dried her hands and grabbed it, half expecting another photo of Nonna Vivi terrorizing Brunella's neighbors.

Instead, it was Giacomo.

"Dimmi," she said.

His voice came through taut. "We have a problem."

She braced herself. "Nonna?"

"Alive," he said. "Too alive. She has organized a neighborhood watch and renamed it 'La Resistenza.'"

"Of course she has," Silvia muttered. "So what's the problem?"

"Marco," he said.

She straightened. "Gelato Marco?"

"Yes. He called." Giacomo lowered his voice, though there was no one to overhear. "Two men came into the shop this morning. Not the usual one with the cheap suit. New. One had a scar on his cheek. They went into the back room, asked him how sales were going. Asked if anyone had been asking questions."

"Was he honest?" Silvia asked.

"He lied," Giacomo said. "He said no one. They didn't believe him. The one with the scar told him there would be 'big expectations' at the event in two days. They want the honey flavor front and center. Special batch. He heard them say something about 'making sure they get a proper taste.'"

Silvia's stomach rolled. "Our antidote isn't ready," she said. "We're close, but we don't know dosage, timing. We can't protect an entire piazza of people."

"That's why I'm calling," Giacomo said. "We need to stop it before they start handing out cups. Or at least… cut the supply. Make it so there's nothing to serve."

"Easier said than done," Silvia said. She paced to the window, staring out at the vines. "We'd have to intercept the trucks. Or sabotage the freezers. Or convince the mayor he's about to co-host a mass poisoning."

"Mayors don't like being made fools of," Giacomo said. "If we had proof—real proof—that the honey is tainted, he might cancel."

"We're working on proof," Silvia said. "But proof takes time. Davide doesn't."

"Then we get creative," Giacomo said. "I'll talk to some people on this side. See if anyone can slow the supply chain. A flat tire here, a delayed shipment there."

"Small delays won't stop an event with sponsors," she said.

"Maybe not," he said. "But we're not just one team anymore, Silvia. There are more of us than there are of them. For now."

89

She pinched the bridge of her nose. "I'll tell the others," she said. "We'll figure out what we can hit from this side."

"And Silvia?" he added.

"Mm?"

"Tell them to be careful in town," he said. "If they went to see Marco, they know. They're watching."

She looked toward the road, as if she could see all the invisible eyes. "We know," she said. "We've already heard from their bullets."

The Shadow in the Street

Cassidy and Adriano stepped out of the parish office into the bright midday glare, the Florence business card hot in Cassidy's pocket.

Her mind buzzed with possibilities.

Elena Valenti in Florence.

La Notte del Miele at the old convent.

The idea that the real antidote might not be ink on a page, but a dish remembered by the people who ate it.

"We need to go to Florence," she said, as they headed back toward the piazza. "Talk to Elena. Ask what they served. See if she has a copy of whatever my mother tore out."

"We will," Adriano said. "But not today."

"Why not today?" she demanded.

"Because we're already targets here," he said. "If we start popping up in multiple cities on the same day asking the same questions, Davide will notice. We need to move like we're smaller than we are."

"That's very Zen of you," she said.

"I'm not Zen," he replied. "I'm paranoid."

They cut through a narrower side street, quieter than the main piazza, lined with shuttered windows and laundry lines. The air felt different here—cooler, echoing.

90

Cassidy's phone buzzed. Lorenzo's photo of the festival poster filled the screen.

She swore. "They're calling it La Notte del Dolce," she said. "Two nights from now. Honey and gelato and music. Sponsored by Davide's brand, of course."

"Of course," Adriano said. He took the phone, scanning the image. "We don't have time to get the antidote perfect before then."

"No," she said. "So we either stop the event or we make sure the honey doesn't arrive."

"Or both," he said.

Her phone buzzed again—Silvia this time, with a quick summary of Giacomo's call. Marco. Men in the back room. A "special batch."

"Special batch," she repeated. "I hate those words."

"They're accelerating," Adriano said. "He's not hiding in the shadows anymore. He's testing how bold he can be."

They walked in silence for a moment.

Then Adriano's hand brushed hers—not casually, but deliberately. "Don't look," he said softly. "But there's a man behind us. Same side of the street. Too close."

Cassidy's pulse jumped, but she kept her gaze forward. "How can you tell he's not just walking?"

"Because he's matching our pace," Adriano said. "And he hasn't looked at a single shop window. Only at us."

"Options?" she asked.

"Left up ahead," he said. "Alley. We take it. If he follows, we have our answer."

"And if he doesn't?"

"Then I owe you a gelato," he said.

"Preferably not laced with toxins."

"Always."

They reached the narrow cross-street, hemmed by stone walls and potted plants. Adriano turned into it without slowing; Cassidy followed, heart hammering. The alley climbed slightly, leading toward a small terrace with a view over the valley.

Footsteps behind them. Not hurried. Just... continuing.

"Still with us?" she asked.

"Yes," Adriano said.

They emerged into the tiny terrace — an overlook with a low stone wall, a bench, and a lone olive tree in a clay pot. No people. No easy exits except the way they'd come and a set of stairs leading down the other side.

Adriano moved to the stone wall, leaning on it as if admiring the view. Cassidy stepped to his side, pretending to fish her phone from her bag.

The man entered the terrace a second later.

He was late thirties, maybe, with a tan that looked cultivated, not earned. Cheap suit. Better shoes than the last goon they'd seen, but still wrong for these streets. He paused when he saw them both facing him, then smiled thinly.

"Buongiorno," he said.

"Beautiful view," Cassidy said brightly. "Is this where we're supposed to pretend we don't recognize you from Siena?"

His smile tightened. "I don't know what you mean."

"Oh, good," she said. "We get to play the lying game."

Adriano's voice dropped. "You've improved your aim since the bakery courtyard," he said. "Kitchen shots were very neat."

The man's gaze flicked toward him, then back to Cassidy. "Just keeping an eye on things," he said. "My employer likes to know who's... stirring the pot."

"Tell your employer the pot was already boiling," Cassidy said. "We're just trying to keep it from spilling on everyone."

He ignored that. "You've been asking many questions," he said. "Pharmacies. Records. Gelato. It's not very discreet."

"Subtlety has never been my strong point," she said.

He took a step closer. "You should stop," he said. "You and your... friends. Go back to Florence. Or wherever you crawled out of. Enjoy your little romances. Write your little articles. Leave the honey to the professionals."

"Poisoning?" she said. "Is that what we're calling it now?"

His eyes cooled. "You don't understand scale," he said. "You think this is about a few jars. A few people. It's not. This is about flow. Control. Who owns sweetness. You think you can fight that with one little notebook and a few flowers?"

"I've seen people fight worse with less," Adriano said.

The man's gaze flicked between them, assessing. Measuring.

"You're not the first who tried to do this," he said to Cassidy. "Your mother thought she could too."

Her throat went dry. "You knew her."

"I knew of her," he said. "She was smarter than you. She knew when to keep her head down. She just... didn't do it often enough."

"What happened to the missing page?" she asked, before she could think better of it.

He smiled faintly. "Ah," he said. "So you've noticed the gap. Good. That means you're at least half as clever as she was." He shrugged. "Pages have a way of ending up where they're most... useful."

"In Davide's hands?" Adriano asked.

"In someone's hands," he said. "Someone who understands that sometimes you can't stop the stream. You can only decide who drowns."

Cassidy stepped forward despite herself. "If you hurt anyone at that festival —"

He cut her off with a small, disdainful laugh. "Hurt?" he said. "I don't hurt people. I move product. If people can't handle it, they shouldn't be eating in the twenty-first century."

"Tell that to the old man in the hospital," she snapped. "The kids with hearts that race for no reason. The people who trusted that little bee on the label."

He spread his hands. "Everyone trusts something," he said. "Some trust a company. Some trust a story. Some trust a dead woman's recipes. Me?" His smile sharpened. "I trust that when the market wants sweetness, someone will supply it. If not me, someone worse."

"You're not—" she began.

"No," he cut in. "I'm not the worst. That's why you're still alive."

Silence thickened.

"Pull back," he said. "You've made your point. You're... annoying. Davide likes to swat flies, not chase them. Be grateful you're still in the fly category."

"And if we don't?" Adriano asked.

The man's smile vanished entirely. "Then gunshots and gelato," he said softly. "In that order."

Cassidy's heart stuttered.

He stepped back, tipped two fingers to his temple in a parody of a salute, and turned to leave. At the edge of the terrace, he paused.

"Oh," he said over his shoulder. "One more thing. Tell your friend Marco to stop playing hero. We don't like heroes in dessert shops."

Cassidy's hands curled into fists. "If you touch him—"

"You don't get to make conditions," he said. "You're already in over your head."

Then he was gone, footsteps receding down the stairs, merging with the murmur of the town.

For a long moment, neither of them spoke.

"Gunshots and gelato," Adriano said at last. "He said it like it was a... slogan."

"Like it's the plan," she said. "Noise and sweetness. Fear and sugar."

She leaned on the stone wall, trying to slow her breathing. The view below swam—a blur of red roofs and green fields and people who had no idea a man in a cheap suit had just threatened to turn their piazza into a test site.

"We can't back off," she said. "Not now. Not when he's saying things like that."

"I know," Adriano said.

"But we also can't let him dictate the terms," she continued, voice low and fierce. "If we spend all our time reacting to his threats, we'll never get ahead."

"Then we set our own terms," he said.

She turned to face him. "We go to Florence," she said. "Soon. Find Elena. Find out what my mother cooked that night. Turn the antidote from a maybe into a yes."

"And for the festival?" he asked.

She exhaled. "We hit him where it hurts," she said. "In his image. In his trust. In his supply. We make it too risky for the mayor to go through with it. We make it so loud—even quietly— that he can't pretend he didn't know."

"Leverage," Adriano said.

"Leverage," she agreed.

Her phone buzzed again—Lorenzo this time, then Silvia, then Giacomo, like a chorus.

She looked at Adriano. "We're in it now," she said. "Deep."

"We were always in it," he replied. "Now we just know how far down it goes."

The Package at the Gate

By the time they made it back to the vineyard, the light had shifted toward late afternoon, the sun slanting lower. The air buzzed with insects and the faint hum of Enrico's radio drifting from the open kitchen window.

Silvia met them halfway up the drive, her expression tight.

"Good news or bad news first?" she asked.

"You choose," Cassidy said wearily.

95

"Good news: we have a name." She held up Elena's card, which Cassidy had texted earlier. "Valenti. Ethical Kitchen. Florence. Very noble. Very annoying."

"And the bad?" Adriano asked.

Silvia jerked her chin toward the gate.

Someone had left a crate there.

It sat just inside the entrance, neat and square, as if delivered by a very polite courier with very impolite intentions. No truck in sight. No dust trail. Just the crate.

From a distance, Cassidy could see the logo burned into the wood: the bee, the drop of honey, the rolling Tuscan hill.

DolceVero.

Her skin crawled.

"We didn't touch it," Silvia said. "Enrico wanted to set it on fire. I told him we should at least see what's inside before we burn it."

Together, they approached.

Up close, the crate looked almost tasteful. The bee logo had been done with care. A paper label on top read, in cheerful script: *UN ASSAGGIO DI DOLCEZZA PER I NOSTRI VICINI – CON AFFETTO.*

A taste of sweetness for our neighbors. With affection.

"Do we have neighbors?" Cassidy asked.

"No," Enrico said, appearing behind them with a shovel. "Just enemies."

"Subtlety is truly dead," Lorenzo muttered.

"Could be a bomb," Silvia said.

"Could be honey," Lorenzo replied.

"Could be both," Cassidy said.

They stood in a small semicircle, staring at it like it might blink.

Finally, Adriano stepped forward. "Everyone back," he said. "Just in case."

He knelt beside the crate, inspecting it. No wires visible, no ticking. Just nailed-in slats and that smug bee.

Using the shovel handle as a lever, he pried one corner up, then another, loosening the top until he could lift it off without putting his face directly above it.

Inside, nestled in straw, were jars.

Half a dozen glass jars of honey and spreads with the DolceVero labels, arranged around a single gelato cup with the Gelato d'Oro logo. Melted residue streaked the cup's inside. On top of them, like a garnish, rested a single spent bullet.

"Charming," Silvia said.

Lorenzo let out a long breath. "Gunshots and gelato," he said. "Gift-wrapped."

Cassidy stared at the bullet, the cup, the jars. Each element a small, symbolic barb: we know what you're doing, we know what you're testing, we know where you sleep.

"They want us scared," she said.

"I am scared," Enrico said. "I am also furious. Fear and fury make a good sauce."

"We can use this," Adriano said, surprising her.

"How?" Cassidy asked.

"As proof," he said. "Not for the police—they'd laugh us out of the station. But for the mayor. For Teresa. For the Keepers. We can show them this is not paranoia. This is targeted intimidation from a company hosting town events."

"And the bullet?" Lorenzo asked.

"We keep it," Adriano said. "Maybe one day, we put it on Davide's table and remind him he missed."

Silence hummed.

Cassidy straightened. "Okay," she said. "So. Recap."

She ticked items off on her fingers.

"We have:

– evidence of tainted honey and gelato,
– a partial antidote that works in a dish,
– a mass event in two days that could become a catastrophe,
– a Florence contact who might hold the missing piece,

– and a cheap-suit messenger who thinks we're still in the fly category."

"And a crate of passive-aggressive poison on our doorstep," Lorenzo added.

"And that," she said.

She looked at each of them in turn—Adriano, jaw set; Lorenzo, restless energy crackling; Silvia, eyes cool and sharp; Enrico, simmering under his apron; Nina, watching them all with canine suspicion, as if ready to attack the bee logo itself.

"We're a third of the way through this," Cassidy thought, the storyteller part of her unable to stop framing it that way. In any other story, this would be the moment where the heroes either pull together or fall apart.

"I vote for pulling together," she said aloud.

"No one asked for a vote," Silvia said. "But yes."

"We split again tomorrow," Adriano said. "Silvia and Lorenzo work on the festival—mayor, permits, threats, whatever leverage we can find. You and I go to Florence. We find Elena. We find out what they cooked at La Notte del Miele. We finish the antidote."

"And I stay here," Enrico said, "make sure no one steals my flour or my dog."

"And if Davide's people decide to escalate?" Lorenzo asked.

"Then," Adriano said, looking at the crate, at the bullet, at the hill beyond, "they find out what happens when you underestimate people who know how to use a kitchen."

Cassidy felt that strange, fierce calm settle over her again.

They were in deep. The web was bigger than they'd thought. The missing page was somewhere between Florence and memory. But they had direction now. Names. Places. A festival countdown ticking louder with each breath.

Somewhere, she thought, her mother was either screaming in frustration or raising a glass.

She hoped it was the latter.

As the sun slid toward the horizon, painting the sky in molten colors, Cassidy looked at the crate one last time and imagined it burning. Not out of fear, but as a prelude.

Gunshots and gelato, she thought.

Fine.

They could play that game.

But they'd be the ones to write the ending.

Chapter 6 – La Notte del Miele (Again)

By the time the sun dragged itself over the hills, the crate was still sitting at the gate like an accusation.

Cassidy couldn't stop looking at it as she drank her coffee on the porch. The bee logo, the neat script, the bullet glinting in its nest of straw—it all felt like a thesis statement from Davide:

I see you.

I know where you sleep.

And I am not subtle.

"You're glaring at it like it's going to apologize," Silvia said, stepping out with her own mug.

"It should," Cassidy said. "At least for the font choice."

"Italy is at war with a psychopath and you're critiquing branding."

"I contain multitudes."

Down in the yard, Enrico was circling the crate with Nina at his heels, muttering darkly under his breath. He'd already threatened to bury it in the vineyard, throw it in the river, and mail it back filled with manure.

"We are not sending feces to a crime syndicate," Lorenzo had said when that last idea surfaced.

"Why not?" Enrico had demanded. "Symbolism."

Now, Lorenzo emerged from the kitchen with a canvas bag and his notebook, hair still damp from the shower, eyes alert.

"Okay," he said briskly. "Festival T-minus forty-eight hours. Team Florence, ready?"

Cassidy swallowed the last of her coffee. "Ready-ish."

Adriano came out behind him, car keys in hand. He'd shaved, which somehow made him look more dangerous, not less.

"Florence today," he said. "Elena. Answers. If we're lucky."

"And here we put pressure on the mayor," Silvia said. "Show him the crate. The bullet. Make it very clear his cheerful honey festival might come with side effects and manslaughter charges."

Enrico snorted. "He will listen," he said. "He is vain, but he is not stupid. His wife will make him listen if we do not."

"Leave the jars in the house for now," Adriano added, nodding toward the crate. "We might need them as evidence."

"Evidence belongs in a courtroom," Enrico said. "Not in my pantry."

"We'll get it out of your pantry as soon as we can," Cassidy said. "Promise."

He sighed, then jabbed a finger at her. "You," he said. "You go to Florence and you do not get shot. Or abducted. Or married."

"That's a weird list," she said.

"In Florence, anything can happen," he replied.

Nina trotted up and pressed her head against Cassidy's leg. Cassidy scratched behind her ears.

"If we're not back by sunset," she told the dog, "go find a terrifying shepherd and form a militia."

Nina wagged her tail solemnly.

A Familiar Road to Florence

The drive to Florence in their borrowed car should have been familiar.

Cassidy had been there so many times before, back in the "normal" part of her Italian life, when Florence had been the center of her universe—her apartment, her job at the magazine, the coffee bar where the barista knew her order, the supermarket where the cashier had called her *tesoro* that one time and she'd almost cried.

Now, every kilometer of the road felt layered. Old memories. New danger.

They passed Siena's turnoff, and Cassidy's stomach remembered the tunnels. A little farther, the landscapes opened into rolling hills and cypress-lined drives, those endlessly photogenic postcard scenes that made people book flights without reading the fine print about organized food crime.

101

"You're quiet," Adriano said after a while.

"Thinking," she said.

"Dangerous habit."

She watched the highway unravel ahead of them—a gray ribbon between fields. "I used to do this drive for dumb reasons," she said. "Deadlines. Weekend trips. A sale at a store that sold plates I couldn't afford."

"And now?" he asked.

"Now I'm doing it because my mother might have hidden the key to an antidote in a dinner party I wasn't invited to, someone tore pages out of her notebook, and a man in a cheap suit just threatened to weaponize a gelato festival."

"So a normal road trip," he said.

She smiled despite herself. "You know what I mean," she said softly. "It's different being a tourist in a place and realizing you were supposed to be… woven into it. That she was weaving you in even when you didn't know it."

He glanced at her, quick and sideways, before returning his eyes to the road. "You were always woven into it," he said. "You just didn't see the threads."

"That's a very poetic way of saying my mother was meddling," she said.

"She was trying to keep you alive," he replied. "She just had a… dramatic way of going about it."

Cassidy traced a circle on the fogged edge of the window with her fingertip. "Do you think," she asked, "she knew it would end like this? That we'd be here, driving to Florence to ask one of her colleagues how to finish something she started?"

"I think," he said slowly, "that she knew she might not be the one to finish it. And she didn't want Davide to be the one who did. So she left pieces. For someone stubborn enough to pick them up."

"Stubborn is a nice word for 'does not take hints,'" she said.

"It's also a nice word for 'does not stop when threatened with bullets,'" he said.

She took a breath. "Do you think Elena will talk to us?" she asked. "If she's still even there?"

"If your mother trusted her enough to loop her into a Keepers dinner, she's not a coward," he said. "Cautious, maybe. But not a coward."

They hit the outskirts of Florence, the traffic densifying as the city closed around them—stringy lines of cars, scooters darting like fish, pedestrians appearing where no pedestrian should logically be.

Florence wasn't a skyline city. It revealed itself sideways: a dome glimpsed between buildings, a tower in a rearview mirror, the sudden shock of the Arno glittering under a bridge.

Cassidy's chest tightened. Images ricocheted: the front door of her old apartment; her desk at the magazine; a certain barstool at a certain café where she'd once sat and thought *I could stay here forever.*

Spoiler: she had not.

"Hey," Adriano said quietly. "You okay?"

"Yes," she said. "No. Ask me again later."

He guided the car into the Oltrarno, the neighborhood south of the river—the side of Florence that always felt more lived-in, less polished. Artisan workshops, narrow streets, laundry overhead. People shouted greetings between open windows. Someone was already burning garlic at ten in the morning.

"This was the address on Anna's card," he said, turning into a lane where the stones seemed older than language.

They pulled up in front of a small doorway with a faded sign: *CUCINA ETICA – LABORATORIO.* Metal shutters covered the windows. A *for rent* notice had been taped crookedly to the wall.

"Great," Cassidy said. "So much for Elena living at the same address for ten years like a normal narrative convenience."

"She's still in Florence," a voice behind them said.

They turned.

A woman in her seventies stood in the doorway of the building next door, watering a plant in a chipped terracotta pot. Her white hair was braided and coiled like a crown. Her eyes were sharp enough to slice bread.

"You know her?" Adriano asked.

"Everyone knew her," the woman said. "She made soup for half this street during Covid." She squinted at Cassidy. "You look like someone."

"I get that a lot," Cassidy said weakly.

"Your mother," the woman said. "She came here once. Tall. Intense. Cooked an entire meal in my kitchen because she didn't trust my food."

"Yes," Cassidy said faintly. "That sounds like her."

The woman nodded, satisfied. "Elena moved two years ago," she said. "The rent went up. The world went mad. She joined a co-op kitchen by Santo Spirito. You look for the door that smells like garlic and revolution."

"Garlic and revolution," Cassidy repeated. "Very helpful. Thank you."

"Tell her," the woman said, "that Bianca says she still hasn't returned my pot."

"I will," Cassidy promised.

Garlic and Revolution

The co-op kitchen turned out to be on a side street near Piazza Santo Spirito, down a hallway that looked like it should lead to a storage closet. Instead, it opened into a high-ceilinged room full of stainless-steel tables, big pots, prep boards, and at least four different arguments about salt happening simultaneously.

"Perfect," Cassidy murmured. "She's upgraded to chaos."

The air was thick with smells—garlic, tomatoes, simmering stock, herbs, bread in some early stage of becoming. A chalkboard near the door listed the day's tasks: Community lunch. Food recovery. Workshop: *Radical Minestrone – Feeding Many with Little.*

"That's… not ominous," Cassidy said.

A woman stood at the far counter, back turned. She was in her mid-fifties, maybe, with short dark hair threaded with silver, sleeves rolled up, forearms dusted with flour. She moved with an economy that said she'd spent decades in kitchens, real ones, not Instagram sets.

"Elena?" Adriano called.

The woman glanced over her shoulder. Her eyes—dark, steady, appraising—took them in quickly: Adriano, then Cassidy, then the fact that they were standing together and not holding a delivery box or a donation.

For a heartbeat, something like recognition flashed across her face. Then she wiped her hands on a towel and walked over, tossing instructions to a younger cook without looking.

"Vitale," she said to Adriano. "I had never met you, but Giulia used to say you show up when things are on fire."

"Only the important fires," he replied.

She turned to Cassidy. Up close, her gaze was almost physically tangible. "You," she said. "You look like Catherine. But younger. Angrier."

Cassidy's throat tightened. "I'm Cassidy," she said. "Her daughter."

Elena nodded once, as if confirming an equation. "You took your time," she said.

"Excuse me?" Cassidy squeaked.

"Your mother assumed it would be you," Elena said. "If anyone came. She said you were stubborn enough. I said you might be smart enough to stay out of it." She shrugged. "Clearly, I lost that argument."

"You… talked about me?" Cassidy asked, feeling bizarrely exposed.

"Constantly," Elena said. "Usually in the context of, 'She doesn't know any of this and she mustn't know until it's safe.'" She tilted her head. "So. I assume it's not safe."

"No," Cassidy said. "It is extremely not safe."

105

Elena sighed. "Then you'd better come to the back," she said. "We don't talk about this near the carrots."

What Was Served

The back room was smaller, lined with shelves of jars, boxes, and neatly labeled containers: lentils, chickpeas, flour, spices. A small table sat in the middle, stained and honest.

Elena closed the door, shutting out the clang and simmer of the main kitchen. The sudden quiet made Cassidy aware of her own breathing.

"Tea?" Elena asked. "Coffee? Wine?"

"It's barely eleven," Adriano said.

"Exactly," Elena replied. "Coffee then."

While she poured, Cassidy tried to assemble words that didn't sound like an accusation or a plea.

"You were at La Notte del Miele," she blurted. "The dinner at Santa Lucia. With my mother. With Giulia. You helped organize the menu."

"Yes," Elena said. "And I'm the one who took the page from the ledger."

Cassidy almost dropped her cup. "You—what?"

Elena sat, wrapped her hands around her own mug. "Let's not pretend you came here to ease in gently," she said. "Catherine told me to remove it if things went bad. They did. I did. You noticed. Good."

Cassidy stared. "You... you tore it out on her orders?"

Elena nodded. "She realized too late that the antidote wasn't just a recipe," she said. "It was a weapon. In the right hands, it saves lives. In the wrong ones, it can be used to control who lives and who dies. Davide understood that faster than she wanted to believe."

Adriano leaned forward. "Davide was already in the picture then?"

Elena's mouth tightened. "He was on the edges," she said. "Back when the Keepers were still one group instead of a family arguing over a will. He started out like all of us—furious about corruption in the food chain. Angry that cheap, bad products were wiping out small producers. But he saw something we didn't, or maybe refused to see." She lifted a shoulder. "He saw profit."

"So he was one of you," Cassidy said slowly. "And then he wasn't."

"Some people thought they could steer him," Elena said. "Use his ambition. Negotiate. Catherine wasn't one of them. She saw where he was going. That's why she wrote the antidote up in detail —to have something to counter whatever he did. But the more complete it got, the more dangerous it became. A full map that anyone could steal."

"So she asked you to take part of it," Adriano said.

"She asked me to hide it somewhere Davide couldn't easily reach," Elena replied. "She knew he'd come for the ledger eventually. She trusted me more than she trusted paper."

Cassidy's pulse thudded. "So you have it?" she asked. "The missing page?"

Elena's gaze sharpened. "No," she said. "I have something better."

Cassidy wanted to scream. "Better than the exact dosing and scaling instructions for an antidote that could stop a mass poisoning?"

"Yes," Elena said calmly. "Because pages burn. Pages can be photographed and copied and lost. Recipes in people's bones are harder to erase." She took a sip of coffee. "What did you think La Notte del Miele was?"

"A Keepers dinner," Adriano said. "A summit. A symbolic act."

"It was a clinical trial," Elena said. "In fancy clothing."

Cassidy sat back slowly. "You... tested the antidote," she said. "On the guests."

107

"Not in a way that hurt them," Elena said quickly. "We designed a menu that paired small doses of a harmless bitter compound with different vehicles—honey, oil, wine, dessert. We wanted to see how the palate registered it, how the body metabolized it. No one walked out sicker than they came in. Some walked out drunker." A faint smile ghosted across her face. "But we learned a lot."

"And the antidote?" Adriano pressed.

"We realized the safest, most effective way to deliver it wasn't as a stand-alone," Elena said. "It was as a counter-flavor. A ghost note. Something that could ride along with the very thing it was neutralizing."

Cassidy's mind jumped ahead. "Honey," she said.

"And dairy," Elena added. "The fat in gelato, in cream, in certain sauces, helps carry it. Helps it coat the mouth, the throat. We created a dessert—honey semifreddo with a drizzle. The drizzle was the key. The semifreddo was the Trojan horse."

Cassidy's head spun. "So the missing page…"

"Is numbers," Elena said. "Ratios. Temperatures. Boring things. It's useful, but it's not unique. The unique part is in here." She tapped her temple. "In my memory. In the hands that stir."

Adriano nodded slowly. "The infusion," he said. "The way the asphodel binds the bitter elements in Davide's compound. We've seen the reaction in the dish. It works. But we don't know how to turn that into something people can consume safely, at scale."

"I do," Elena said. "Because Catherine made me promise to know. In case someone like you showed up carrying her eyes and her temper."

Cassidy's laugh came out strangled. "No pressure," she said.

Elena leaned back. "You've already started," she said. "You have the base. You have the asphodel. You've seen it bind in small dishes. What you don't have are the tolerances. The limits. How much is enough. How much is too much. How to fold it into something sweet without turning people off with bitterness. How to work with different strengths of contamination. That's what the trial at Santa Lucia was for."

"And you remember?" Adriano asked.

"Not every number," she said. "But enough. Enough to recreate what we did that night. Enough to refine it now, with your asphodel and your tainted honey." She looked at Cassidy. "Enough to make something you can slip into a festival without people spitting it out."

Cassidy's heart jolted. "The festival," she breathed. "La Notte del Dolce. Two nights from now. They're planning a 'special batch' of honey gelato. Free samples everywhere in the piazza."

Elena closed her eyes briefly. "Of course they are," she murmured. "He's nothing if not theatrical."

"If we can get our antidote into the same supply chain," Adriano said, thinking aloud, "or into something people will eat *instead…*"

"We could blunt the damage," Cassidy finished. "Maybe even stop it."

"Not stop," Elena corrected. "Mitigate. Limit. Nothing is perfect. But we can stack the deck back in our favor."

Silence settled, thick and alive.

"Will you help us?" Cassidy asked quietly. "Come to the vineyard. Work with what we have. Help us get this right before he turns our piazza into a lab."

Elena watched her for a long moment. In that gaze, Cassidy felt weighed, measured, cross-examined. Not by a stranger, but by someone who had loved her mother enough to risk defying her once.

"You sound like her," Elena said finally. "And nothing like her. That's probably a good thing." She exhaled. "Yes. I'll come."

Cassidy's chest loosened in a rush. "Thank you," she said, the words feeling too small.

"Don't thank me yet," Elena said. "We still have to steal time from a man who thinks he owns it."

Ghosts in the Refectory

"Before we go," Elena said, "we stop at Santa Lucia."

"The convent?" Adriano asked. "You think there's anything left there?"

"Maybe," she said. "Not of the paper. That's gone. But of the night. Sometimes places remember things even when people don't."

Cassidy wasn't entirely sure whether Elena meant that metaphorically or not. At this point, she wasn't sure it mattered.

They took Enrico's car again, weaving out of the city and up into the hills on a smaller, twistier road than the one they'd taken from Montaione. Florence receded behind them; the landscape turned to olive groves and cypress, stone houses, low stone walls marking old boundaries.

After about twenty minutes, Elena pointed ahead. "There," she said. "On the ridge."

The convent came into view—a cluster of pale buildings, their red roofs dull with age, perched on a small rise. A bell tower stood at one end, stark against the sky, its bell long since removed. Weeds sprouted between some of the stones. Parts of it looked peaceful. Parts of it looked abandoned.

"And people get married here?" Cassidy asked. "For romance?"

"People will get married anywhere with decent parking," Elena said.

A rusted chain hung across the gravel drive, more symbolic than effective. A small sign read: *PRIVATE PROPERTY – EVENT ACCESS ONLY.*

"Elena, if we get arrested for breaking and entering a holy site —" Adriano began.

"It was deconsecrated," Elena said, stepping out of the car. "And the only person who ever checks on it is the caretaker, who is currently in Sicily visiting his sister. I know because he sleeps at the bar where my ex works every Thursday."

"That was a very specific sentence," Cassidy said.

"Welcome to my life," Elena replied. She ducked under the chain. "Come on."

Inside the gates, the air shifted—quieter, thicker, like stepping into a room mid-whisper. The courtyard was overgrown but not wild; someone had weeded in the last few months. The refectory building ran along one side, long and low.

As they approached, the sense of déjà vu pressed at Cassidy's chest. She hadn't been here before, but some part of her—some narrative bone—recognized it.

"This is where she cooked," she said, more to herself than anyone.

Elena glanced at her. "Yes," she said simply.

The refectory doors were locked, but the lock itself was old and uninterested. Elena produced a key ring from her bag.

"You have keys to an abandoned convent," Cassidy said. "Just casually."

"I cater weddings," Elena said. "Sometimes the bride is late, sometimes the priest is late, sometimes the keys are late. I learned to solve one of those problems."

The door creaked open.

Inside, the refectory was a long rectangular hall—high ceiling with wooden beams, walls bare except for the faint outlines of where religious paintings used to hang. A row of windows on one side let in milky light. Spiders had claimed most of the corners.

In the middle of the room, long tables and benches waited like patient ghosts.

Cassidy stepped inside and the air wrapped around her. She could almost hear echoes—voices, laughter, the clink of cutlery, the scrape of chairs.

Elena walked to a spot near the far wall, halfway down the length of the room. "She stood here," she said. "Catherine. To plate

111

the dessert. We set up a station so she could watch everyone's faces as they tasted it."

Cassidy closed her eyes. Her mother appeared in her mind's eye — not from childhood memories, but from the photos she'd found later: hair pulled back, sleeves rolled, expression caught between intensity and amusement. She could see her here, moving between tables, checking reactions, listening.

"What did they say?" Cassidy asked.

"About the dessert?" Elena shrugged. "The usual nonsense people say when they're being polite. 'So interesting.' 'Such depth.' 'I can taste the history.'" She rolled her eyes. "But their bodies talked louder. You could see it in their shoulders. Their breathing. No one grimaced at the bitterness. The drizzle did its job. The binding worked. If there had been poison in their honey, most of it would have been neutralized before it reached their bloodstream."

"And Davide was there," Adriano said.

"Yes," she said. "Watching like a man measuring competitors. He tasted everything. Twice. He knew exactly what Catherine had built."

"And that's when it fractured," Adriano murmured.

"That's when some of us realized," Elena corrected, "that we weren't all fighting for the same endgame. We wanted clean food, accessible to everyone. He wanted leverage. A way to decide who got clean and who didn't."

Cassidy opened her eyes. "Is there anything... concrete left?" she asked. "Notes, markings, anything that might help us now?"

Elena hesitated. "There was a backup," she said. "Not of the full page, but of the key ratios. Catherine didn't trust her own paranoia, so she had me copy a few critical points onto a separate sheet and hide it. 'In case I get hit by a car,' she said. Very cheerful woman."

"And you hid it here?" Adriano asked.

"Yes," Elena said. "Behind the third stone from the corner under the serving table. Very traditional." She walked to the indicated spot and knelt, fingers feeling along the wall.

112

Cassidy and Adriano joined her.

The stone was still there. But when Elena pried it away, the space behind it was empty.

"No," she said.

"Maybe it fell," Cassidy said.

They reached in. Dust. A spider. Nothing else.

Elena sat back hard on the floor. "He's been here," she said.

"Davide?" Adriano asked.

"Or one of his," she said. "The caretaker wouldn't bother. No one else knew where it was. Catherine's dead. Giulia's dead. The only people who knew were me... and the ones who watched too closely that night."

They sat in the quiet for a moment, the emptiness in the hollow feeling bigger than its size.

Cassidy's phone buzzed.

She slipped it out of her pocket. A message from Lorenzo: a photo of the festival poster again, this time annotated with arrows and notes: *stage here, honey booth here, gelato stall here, power boxes here.* Underneath:

Mayor is rattled but trapped. Contracts signed. He can't cancel without losing face and money. Best he'll do is "extra controls." We've got access to the layout. We can create "technical problems" if we need to. How's Florence?

She typed back:

Found Elena. She has antidote in her head. Missing backup is gone. Convent visited. He's ahead of us. But we're catching up. Coming back with secret weapon.

She hesitated, then added:

Also, tell Marco not to be alone in the shop if he can help it. Our cheap-suit friend mentioned him by name.

113

Planning Around a Ghost

They drove back toward Florence in a silence that wasn't entirely empty. Each of them traced different lines in their heads—roads, recipes, risks.

At a small café near the edge of the city, they stopped to regroup. It was one of those unremarkable places locals loved: plastic chairs, burnt coffee smell, TV in the corner showing a game with the volume off.

Elena spread a paper napkin on the table and drew a rough pie chart with a ballpoint pen.

"Let's break this festival down," she said. "We have three fronts."

"Only three," Cassidy muttered. "Luxury."

"One: prevention," Elena said, ignoring her. "Stopping or reducing exposure. That means limiting how much of Davide's honey and gelato people actually ingest."

"Lorenzo and Silvia," Adriano said. "They're already working the mayor. They have some leverage. They can maybe cut power to some stalls. Cause delays. Create 'technical problems' the day of."

"Good," Elena said. She drew an X. "Two: mitigation. For the people who do eat it anyway. We need something we can give them—quickly, quietly—that blunts the poison in real time."

"Our antidote dessert," Cassidy said. "Or drink. Or drizzle. Something we can serve without a permit and without getting arrested."

"Exactly," Elena said. "Something 'artisanal' and free. Italians rarely say no to free."

She shaded another section of the napkin. "Three: exposure," she said. "Not of people to poison, but of Davide to light. If we can gather enough proof—samples, reactions, maybe even a visible incident where someone's symptoms reverse after our intervention—we can blow his brand out of the shadows."

114

"And he knows it," Adriano said. "That's why he's sending bullets and crates. He doesn't fear us as people. He fears the story we could tell."

Cassidy tapped the napkin. "To do any of this, we need the antidote finished," she said. "Tested. Dosed. We need to know how much to give a child versus an adult. How quickly it acts. How long it lasts."

"I can help with that," Elena said. "We'll need a long night. A lot of coffee. And some volunteers."

"Not actual people," Cassidy said quickly.

Elena smiled faintly. "Calm down," she said. "I mean volunteers from the plant world. Onions. Egg whites. Classic binders. If we can see how the antidote sticks to proteins in a controlled environment, we can extrapolate."

"Still sounds like potions," Cassidy muttered.

"Medicine is potions," Elena said. "Doctors just hate the word."

Adriano checked his watch. "If we leave now, we can be back at the vineyard before dark," he said. "We can start tonight. Tomorrow we refine. The day after..." He didn't finish.

"The day after, we go to a party," Cassidy said. "Worst party ever."

Elena looked at her, eyes thoughtful. "Your mother thought she had time," she said quietly. "She thought Davide would move slower. That she could build quietly in the background, get everything perfect before stepping out. She was wrong."

Cassidy swallowed. "And me?" she asked. "What do you think I have?"

"Less time," Elena said. "More allies. And a better sense of when to shout."

Cassidy huffed a laugh. "That's one way to put it."

Florence in the Rearview

115

Leaving Florence felt different this time.

Cassidy watched the city slip away through the passenger window—the dome shrinking, the bridges flattening into lines, the familiar skyline turning into a memory with traffic.

She thought of all the versions of herself that had walked those streets. The one who'd first arrived with two suitcases and a fantasy. The one who'd fallen in love with Italy's light and food and contradictions. The one who'd almost given up and gone home when rent hikes and bureaucracy had piled up.

None of them had imagined this.

"You're very quiet again," Adriano said.

"I'm processing," she said. "It's a new hobby."

He glanced in the rearview mirror at Elena, who had dozed off in the back seat, head tilted against the window, arms folded. "She's something," he said.

"Yeah," Cassidy said. "Part of me wants to hug her. Part of me wants to yell at her for not calling me when she tore out that page."

"She was following your mother's orders," he reminded her.

"I know," she said. "I just… there's a version of my life where she called. Where she said, 'Hey, your mom's in some deep shit with honey pirates. Maybe you want in.'"

"Would you have said yes?" he asked.

"At the time?" She considered. "Probably not. I liked my safe stories. My neatly packaged narratives. I would have told myself I cared by writing about farmers markets instead."

"And now?" he asked.

"Now I don't get to say no," she said. "Now 'in' is where we live."

He reached across the gearshift and found her hand. His fingers threaded through hers easily, as if they'd been doing this for years instead of months, lifetimes, whatever this had become.

"We get to choose how we're in, though," he said. "That's something."

She squeezed his hand. "Do we ever get to be out?" she asked.

"Yes," he said. "When Davide is on trial or in a hole and you're arguing with a barista about milk temperature."

She smiled. "That sounds nice."

"It will happen," he said. "Or something like it. We have to believe that, or we start making desperate choices."

"Like poisoning an entire festival to make a point," she said.

"Exactly," he said. "We're not him. We can't become him to beat him."

The road unspooled before them, familiar now, but charged.

In the back seat, Elena stirred and sat up, blinking. "Wake me up when we're near the vineyard," she said. "I want to see if your hills look as dramatic as Catherine described them."

"She talked about the hills?" Cassidy asked.

Elena smiled faintly. "She talked about everything," she said. "Except the parts that hurt. Those she buried under recipes."

The Mayor's Line in the Sand

Back at the vineyard, the light had softened into late afternoon gold. The rows of vines glowed; the farmhouse looked like a postcard again, which Cassidy had learned was code for "something terrible is about to happen."

Silvia and Lorenzo were waiting in the yard. They both looked like people who had spent the day forcing information out of reluctant bureaucrats.

"Well?" Silvia said, hands on hips. "Does Florence still exist?"

"Barely," Cassidy said. "We brought back an Elena."

Elena stepped out of the car. Lorenzo blinked.

"You didn't warn us you were bringing a legend," he said.

"Legend?" Elena said dryly. "I'm medium height at best."

"We have a lot to tell you," Adriano said. "And you have things to tell us. But first—what did the mayor say?"

117

Lorenzo's mouth did a complicated thing. "He said many words," he said. "Most of them were about liability."

Silvia stepped in. "He can't cancel the festival," she said. "Or rather, he *won't*. The contracts are signed, the sponsors are leaning on him, the regional tourist board is watching. If he tries to pull the plug without something he can show on TV as undeniable, he loses his career."

"So we bite him with a jar," Enrico muttered from the porch.

"He's not entirely useless," Lorenzo said. "We showed him the crate. The bullet. We hinted at what would happen if videos leaked of children collapsing after eating honey under his banner. He went pale. He agreed to three things."

"One," Silvia said, holding up a finger, "he'll allow 'extra health and safety inspections' before the event. That means we get access to the stalls before they open. We can test samples, if we're fast."

"Two," Lorenzo continued, "he gave us the full layout for the festival, including power lines, truck access, and emergency routes. If we have to kill the lights or the fridges, we know which cables to trip."

"And three," Silvia said, "he agreed—off the record—that if we bring him undeniable proof that DolceVero's honey is tainted *before* the second night, he'll shut down their stalls and publicly distance the town from them. He won't say 'poison.' But he will say 'precautionary measures.'"

"It's something," Adriano said.

"It's a very politician something," Elena said. "Enough to protect him. Not enough to protect everyone else."

"We also talked to the fire brigade chief," Lorenzo added. "Turns out he hates the idea of flammable festival decorations near overloaded power strips. We might have an ally if we need one."

Cassidy exhaled. "So we have a window," she said. "A small, fragile window between 'festival starts' and 'people start collapsing.' We use that window to: one, test on the spot; two, deliver the antidote; and three, gather enough proof to force a shutdown."

"The kind of proof that stands up to lawyers," Silvia said.

"And the kind that spreads faster than Davide can spin it," Cassidy added. "Photos. Videos. People telling each other not to eat the honey."

"Gossip," Elena said. "Oldest weapon."

"Second oldest," Lorenzo murmured.

The Long Night Begins

They moved into the kitchen like a small, well-practiced army.

Elena took over the antidote station with the authority of someone who had once orchestrated a dinner that doubled as a clandestine clinical trial. Lorenzo laid out the tainted honey, the gelato samples, the asphodel infusion they'd already developed. Adriano set up burners, water baths, thermometers. Silvia sharpened pencils for notes like they were knives.

Cassidy watched for a moment, then rolled up her sleeves. "Tell me what to do," she said.

"Cut these bulbs," Elena said, sliding a bowl of asphodel roots toward her. "Thin slices. Even. No heroics. We want surface area, not art."

"Yes, chef," Cassidy said.

As she sliced, Elena talked—not in lectures, but in a running commentary that knit together science and instinct.

"The compound Davide is using," she said, "has a bitter signature that clings to metal ions. We can't remove it entirely without stripping the honey of everything that makes it honey. But we can bind enough of it that the body can handle the rest. Think of it like... mopping up a spill so it doesn't reach the door."

"The asphodel infusion is the mop," Lorenzo said.

"Yes," Elena said. "And fat is the handle. The more surface it can coat, the better. That's why gelato is such an effective carrier— for good and for evil."

They tested small batches first.

Dish after dish, they combined controlled amounts of tainted honey, asphodel infusion, and different dairy bases: cream, milk, yogurt. They heated, cooled, stirred, sniffed.

Each time they saw the now-familiar reaction—the thickening, the subtle darkening, the bubble pattern—they noted it. They started timing how quickly the metallic scent faded. They adjusted proportions. They experimented with adding citrus, with varying the heat.

"Too acidic and we denature the honey," Elena muttered over one failed attempt. "Too little and the binder doesn't activate fully. It's like dating. Everyone wants balance, no one knows how to get it."

As the sky outside went from blue to violet to black, the kitchen filled with the smell of sugar, herbs, and something else—hope, maybe, diluted with exhaustion.

At one point, Nina wandered in, sniffed a sample, sneezed dramatically, and stomped out.

"Harsh critic," Cassidy said.

"She prefers sausages," Enrico said.

Around midnight, they hit something like a breakthrough.

Elena held up a spoonful of a new batch—a thick, glossy drizzle the color of amber tea. It smelled... right. The metallic undertone was there, but muted, wrapped in citrus and something floral. When she let a drop fall into a test dish of tainted honey, they watched the reaction ripple outward, bubbles popping at a faster rate than before.

"This," she said. "This is close."

"How close?" Adriano asked.

"If someone ate a moderate amount of Davide's honey," she said, "and we got this into their system within an hour, I'd bet my best pan we'd neutralize enough to keep them out of the hospital."

"And if it's a child?" Cassidy asked.

Elena's gaze didn't waver. "We'd halve the dose," she said. "Twice, spaced out. More gentle on the body."

"And if they ate a lot?" Lorenzo said.

"We'd need more data," she admitted. "More tests. But we don't have time. So we do what we can with what we have."

They kept going.

By two in the morning, they had a working recipe for the drizzle, written down in two different hands and memorized by at least three minds.

By three, they'd tested how it behaved when mixed into cold cream, when swirled into plain gelato base, when drizzled over toast, fruit, plain yogurt. It held.

"It's not perfect," Elena said, staring at the last dish like it might still betray her. "There will be edge cases. People with allergies. People who ate too much, too fast. But it's something."

"It's a lot," Cassidy said. "It's more than we had this morning."

Elena nodded, then pointed with her spoon. "Now we scale," she said. "We need enough for... how many people? In a worst-case scenario."

Lorenzo did a quick mental calculation. "If the piazza is full, maybe two thousand spread over two nights," he said. "But not all of them will eat the honey. Some will go for chocolate. Some will skip dessert."

"Optimist," Silvia said.

"So we plan for half," Elena said. "Enough drizzle for a thousand portions, at least. If we embed it in something people will want to eat even without knowing it's saving their lives..."

"Like what?" Enrico asked. "We cannot just stand in the piazza and pour it into their mouths. People will think it is a religious cult."

"We make our own stall," Cassidy said, the idea blooming even as she spoke. "A 'community dessert' stand. Free tastings.

121

Something simple. Something that doesn't require refrigeration or permits from five different agencies."

"Granita," Adriano said suddenly.

Everyone turned to him.

He shrugged. "My grandmother used to make lemon granita for summer festivals," he said. "Crushed ice, sugar, lemon juice. Easy to prepare in large quantities. Refreshing. People crave it in crowds."

"And we can fold the drizzle in," Elena said slowly. "A measured amount in each batch. The ice will keep it stable for hours. The lemon will help carry the flavor and mask any bitterness."

"We'll need machines," Lorenzo said. "Or at least big tubs and strong arms."

"We have both," Enrico said. "And neighbors who owe me favors."

"We can brand it as a 'solidarity stand,'" Cassidy said, her journalist brain sparking in a different direction now. "Proceeds—if we even charge—for local producers affected by cheap imports. It fits the narrative. It doesn't scream 'secret antidote to industrial poison.'"

"And if we get questioned?" Silvia asked.

"We say we're activists with good PR," Cassidy said. "Which is basically true."

They worked until their hands shook and their brains stuttered.

By the time the first gray light of dawn crept around the edges of the shutters, they had:

– a large stock of asphodel infusion
– a batch of concentrated drizzle that could be scaled up
– a rough recipe for lemon granita with embedded antidote
– a list of equipment they'd need to beg, borrow, or steal
– and a festival map covered in circles and arrows, now sticky with honey stains.

Cassidy stood in the doorway for a moment, watching the sky lighten over the vines.

Her body ached. Her eyes burned. Her heart felt like someone had been using it as a stress ball.

But under all of that, something else hummed.

They had moved.

Davide had sent bullets and crates and threats.

They had answered with recipes.

A Call from the Edge

As everyone started dribbling off toward showers or collapsing sideways on couches, Cassidy's phone buzzed again.

Giacomo.

She stepped outside to answer, the dawn chill biting at her sweat-damp neck.

"Dimmi," she said.

His voice was low, but she could hear tension vibrating under it. "We have a problem," he said. "Again."

"Please be a small problem," she said.

"Marco didn't show up to open the gelato shop this morning," Giacomo said. "No one can reach him. His phone is off. His apartment is empty."

The world seemed to tilt.

"Empty how?" she asked carefully.

"Empty like he left in a hurry," Giacomo said. "Neighbors heard a car in the middle of the night. Voices. A door slam. No one saw his face."

Cassidy's hand tightened around the phone. "You think they took him."

"I think," Giacomo said slowly, "that men who threaten heroes in dessert shops don't make idle promises."

She swallowed. "We're almost ready," she said. "With the antidote. With a plan for the festival."

"Good," he said. "Because Davide just raised the stakes. Again."

She closed her eyes briefly.

"Tell Nonna we're working," she said. "Tell her we're going to make his sweetness choke him."

Giacomo exhaled something that might have been a laugh. "She says she expects nothing less," he said. "And that if you let him ruin gelato, she will haunt you personally."

"Deal," Cassidy said.

She hung up and stood there for a long moment, letting the cold air slap her fully awake.

Marco was gone. Whether he was still alive, they didn't know. The festival clock ticked louder.

The missing page wasn't paper anymore. It stood in their kitchen, drinking coffee, measuring sugar.

They had eighty-something hours of work behind them.

Forty-eight before the piazza filled.

She turned back toward the house, where Adriano was leaning in the doorway, watching her.

"Well?" he asked.

"Marco's missing," she said. "Taken, most likely."

He swore softly.

She stepped closer, until they were almost touching. "We have to make this count," she said. "Not just for the abstract 'people.' For him. For everyone who didn't get a choice."

He reached up and brushed a streak of honey from her wrist she hadn't noticed. "We will," he said. "We don't stop now."

She looked past him, into the kitchen where jars, bowls, spoons, and notes were scattered like the aftermath of a very precise storm.

Chapter six, she thought, if her life were still a book in neat arcs.

The part where the pieces fall into place just enough to see the shape of the ending.

Now they just had to survive writing it.

Chapter 7 – Lemon, Lies, and Lines in the Sand

The second dawn in a row found everyone at the vineyard looking like they'd been marinated in coffee and bad decisions.

Cassidy sat at the kitchen table, elbows braced on the wood, watching the thin column of steam curl up from her mug like it was trying to escape too. Her hands still smelled faintly of lemon and honey from the night before. Her brain still hummed with ratios, grams, milliliters.

The only person who looked remotely awake was Elena.

Of course.

She moved around the stove with steady efficiency, sliding a pan of scrambled eggs onto the counter, tossing a heel of bread into the oven to crisp. Her hair was pinned back, apron already on, eyes clear.

"You slept?" Cassidy asked, incredulous.

"I rested," Elena said. "You don't sleep when you're calibrating something like this. You doze with purpose."

"That's not better," Cassidy muttered.

Across the table, Lorenzo yawned so wide his jaw cracked. Silvia snatched the spoon out of his hand before he stirred honey into his coffee by autopilot.

"Absolutely not," she said. "Until we finish testing, we don't consume any of that in pure form. New house rule."

Lorenzo blinked down at the spoon. "Right," he said. "Poison."

Enrico stomped in from the yard, radio tucked under one arm like a football. "They're already talking about the festival on the local station," he announced. "Interviews, songs, lies. It's like Christmas but with more diabetes."

"Anything useful?" Adriano asked, pouring himself coffee.

"Mayor says it will be 'a celebration of local sweetness,'" Enrico said. "He used the word 'pure' three times. I turned it off so I didn't throw the radio into the pig trough we don't have."

"We can't stop him from playing host," Silvia said. "But we can make sure his guests have options."

Cassidy pulled the festival map closer, the paper now soft at the edges from overhandling. The gelato stall and honey booth were circled in red. Their proposed granita stand had been penciled in nearer the center—an X labeled *SOLIDARITY / GRANITA*.

"We still need permission to be there," she said. "Even as some kind of community stand. The mayor might have given us leeway, but the festival committee will want forms and signatures and blood types."

"I'll deal with them," Lorenzo said. "They like me."

"They like your cooking," Silvia corrected. "But yes. They will listen to you more than they will listen to me telling them their event is a slow-motion health crisis."

"And we need equipment," Elena said. "Ice machines, tubs, freezers, a generator. If we rely on the festival's power and Davide decides to… accidentally unplug us, we lose half our strategy."

Enrico cracked his knuckles. "I know people," he said.

"You always know people," Cassidy said.

"That's because I talk to them," he replied. "You should try it. Instead of writing about them later."

Lemon Logistics

By mid-morning, the vineyard had turned into something between a clandestine catering operation and a resistance camp.

Lorenzo and Silvia headed into Montaione with a folder full of hastily printed forms, a prototype granita recipe, and what Silvia called "our most innocent faces."

"Use your sad eyes," she told Lorenzo as they walked to the car. "You know—the 'I just want to support local farmers' look."

"I don't have sad eyes," he protested.

"You absolutely do," Cassidy said. "It's infuriating."

"I'll weaponize them responsibly," he promised.

126

Enrico, meanwhile, marched off down the hill with a list in one hand and a rolled-up extension cord over his shoulder, Nina trotting at his side like a furry deputy.

"Where's he going?" Cassidy asked.

"To terrorize the neighbors," Adriano said. "In the name of equipment."

"He'll start with the restaurant on the next hill," Elena added. "They owe him for that time he fixed their oven with duct tape and prayer."

Cassidy imagined Enrico appearing in various kitchens like a wrathful god of pesto, demanding granita machines and spare freezers "for the good of the people." It comforted her more than it should have.

That left her, Adriano, and Elena in the kitchen with the drizzle, the asphodel infusion, and a list of tests they hadn't yet had time to run.

"We've proven it binds in controlled dishes," Elena said, tapping the notebook. "Now we need to see how it behaves with different concentrations of the toxin. We know Davide's compound dosage varies—cheaper jars might be lighter, premium ones heavier. If we only calibrate for one scenario, we're blind to the others."

"How do we test that without a lab?" Cassidy asked.

Elena shrugged. "We fake a lab," she said. "We make three different concentrations of tainted honey—low, medium, high— based on what you've seen so far. Then we apply the drizzle in varying ratios to each, measure the reaction time, and infer."

"That's... very hand-wavy," Cassidy said.

"It's cooking," Elena said. "And chemistry. Both involve educated guesses under pressure."

They got to work.

By noon, they had a series of labeled dishes lined up on the counter like a row of strange, sticky soldiers.

A: low contamination, no antidote.
B: low contamination, drizzle at 1:5 ratio.
C: low contamination, drizzle at 1:3.
D: medium contamination, no antidote.
E: medium contamination, drizzle 1:5.
F: medium contamination, drizzle 1:3.
G: high contamination, no antidote.
H: high contamination, drizzle 1:3.
I: high contamination, drizzle 1:2.

They watched, sniffed, timed the fading of the metallic scent, the changing viscosity.

"It's not an exact science," Elena conceded, "but we can see trends. Lower doses neutralize faster, as expected. Even the higher ones show significant binding at 1:3. 1:2 starts to risk overwhelming the base flavor—people would notice something 'off'."

"So we aim for a conservative drizzle amount in the granita," Adriano said. "Enough to catch most realistic exposures, without making anyone suspect we're feeding them medicine."

"And for people who are already symptomatic?" Cassidy asked. "The farmer at the hospital. The kids with racing hearts. People at the festival who've been eating this stuff for months."

"For them, we may need more targeted doses," Elena said. "A direct spoonful, under the guise of... what do you call it? 'Herbal remedy.' 'Old family cure.' Italians love those. They'll drink anything if you tell them your Nonna invented it."

"So we have granita for the crowd," Cassidy summarized, "drizzle-and-yogurt shots for anyone who looks like they might keel over, and a prayer for everyone else."

"Sounds like a war," Elena said.

"It is," Adriano said.

Market Tests

In the early afternoon, Sylvia's phone buzzed with a message from the pharmacist.

Rinaldi.

Can you come? I have someone you should meet. And something you should see.

They met her in the back room of the pharmacy — a small space with a desk, shelves of forms, and a window that looked out on a narrow alley dominated by a fig tree.

Rinaldi closed the door behind them. "I can't keep doing this without understanding what's happening," she said, voice low. "People trust me. They come here first, before the hospital. I need more than 'stress' to tell them."

"We're working on that," Cassidy said. "Slowly."

"I brought someone," Rinaldi said. "He agreed to talk to you. And to... test something. It was his idea, actually."

She opened the door to the store area and called, "Prego."

An older man stepped inside. Late sixties, maybe, with the build of someone who'd spent his life lifting things heavier than himself. His hair was more white than black now, his skin weathered, his eyes bright but tired.

"This is Signor De Luca," Rinaldi said. "The farmer I mentioned. The one who... changed."

"You're the ones asking about the honey," De Luca said without preamble. "And the trucks."

"Yes," Cassidy said. "We think the honey might be making people sick. We're trying to undo it."

He nodded once. "I figured," he said. "Rinaldi doesn't call people in for tea."

"How have you been feeling?" Adriano asked, though he could guess.

"Wrong," De Luca said. "Not all the time. But enough. Heart kicking like a mule after nothing. Head foggy. Hands jittery." He held them out; they trembled faintly. "Doctor says my tests are fine.

129

My wife says I'm lazy. I say..." He shrugged. "I don't know what I say."

"You eat the bee honey," Cassidy said gently.

He snorted. "I eat all honey," he said. "My brother keeps bees. I kept bees. We all keep bees. But lately everyone buys the cheap jars from the supermarket. My son brought some home—'Look, Papa, Italian brand, good price.' I didn't think twice. Why would I?"

Rinaldi's mouth tightened. "He brought one of the jars," she said. "I compared it. It tasted... off. I thought I was imagining it."

"You weren't," Adriano said.

De Luca looked between them. "Rinaldi says you have something," he said. "A way to make it... less bad."

"The beginning of something," Cassidy said. "We don't have formal trials or official approval or any of the things that make this feel safe in a brochure. But we've seen it work on the compound in dishes. We think it would help."

"I'm not asking for a guarantee," he said. "I'm asking for a chance not to feel like my own heart is trying to outrun me."

Silence hummed for a moment.

Elena stepped forward from where she'd been leaning against the shelf, arms crossed. "We brought a small dose," she said. "Mixed in yogurt. It's not poison. It's herbs and citrus and a binding agent made from a flower that's been growing around here longer than any of us. Worst case, you think it tastes strange and it doesn't do much. Best case..." She spread her hands. "You feel a little more like yourself."

De Luca considered her. "Were you at that dinner at the convent?" he asked suddenly. "Years ago. My cousin cooked for it. Came back talking about 'ethical menus' and 'food as medicine.'"

"Yes," Elena said.

130

He nodded, as if that decided something. "Then I'll try it," he said. "If you were brave enough to annoy the Church, you're brave enough for this."

They sat him at the tiny desk, heart monitor clip from Rinaldi's kit attached to his finger. She took baseline readings—pulse, blood pressure, oxygen.

"High," she murmured. "As usual."

Elena opened a small jar and spooned out a portion of yogurt with the drizzle folded in. It looked harmless. Mild. It smelled faintly of lemon and honey and something green.

Cassidy watched De Luca lift the spoon, her own pulse thudding in her throat.

He hesitated only briefly, then ate.

They waited.

One minute. Three. Five.

Rinaldi watched the monitor like a hawk. Cassidy watched De Luca's face.

At first, nothing changed. He cracked a weak joke about the taste—"I've had worse at health spas"—trying to ease the tension.

Then, around the seven-minute mark, something shifted.

His shoulders, which had been bunched near his ears, relaxed a fraction. His hands steadied on his knees. His breathing slowed.

Rinaldi's eyes widened. "Heart rate dropping," she said. "Not into danger territory. Into… normal."

"How do you feel?" Adriano asked quietly.

De Luca blinked, like he was waking from a light sleep. "Like someone turned down a radio in the next room," he said. "It's been buzzing for months. I didn't realize how loud it was until now."

Cassidy's eyes stung.

"It might not last forever," Elena cautioned. "We don't know how long the effect holds. But if it buys you clearer hours, days… it's something."

De Luca stood slowly, testing his balance. "Whatever you're cooking," he said, "keep cooking it. And if anyone tells you this is

131

a bad idea, send them to my fields. I'll show them what 'bad' looks like."

Rinaldi pressed a hand to her mouth, then let out a shaky laugh.

"I can't write a prescription for this," she said. "But I can... advise people to visit a certain 'solidarity stand' at the festival."

"Is that ethical?" Cassidy asked.

Rinaldi gave her a look. "Ethical?" she echoed. "We're trying to save people from a man who thinks they are acceptable collateral. I'll risk a strongly worded letter from the medical board."

They left with more than they'd brought: anecdotal, yes—but real. Evidence that, in at least one living body, the drizzle did something good.

"Catherine would have loved this," Elena said quietly as they stepped back into the square. "Not the situation. The hack. Taking something meant for harm and twisting it back."

"She would have loved the part where we validated it in a human," Cassidy said. "She was a scientist. She hated theory without data."

"She also hated being wrong," Elena said. "She would have been insufferably pleased right now."

Cassidy smiled, then checked her watch. "We need to get back," she said. "If we're going to scale up before tomorrow night, we have to start now."

Neighbors and Machines

By the time they returned to the vineyard, the front yard looked like an appliance graveyard.

Two old granita machines sat near the porch—big, scratched, but functional. A third, sleeker one leaned against a barrel, its plug coiled like a sleeping snake. There were also three chest freezers, one generator, and a mysterious metal tub that looked like it had once been part of a cow.

132

Enrico stood in the middle of it all, arms folded, looking deeply satisfied.

"You robbed a catering warehouse," Cassidy said.

"I borrowed," he corrected. "From friends. From cousins. From enemies who owe me favors."

"How did you convince them?" she asked.

He shrugged. "I told them if their children died from bad honey because they didn't lend me their machines, I would haunt them forever."

"That seems effective," she said.

"We also have a spot confirmed at the festival," Lorenzo called from the porch. "Solidarity stand, right in the central lane. Officially: raising awareness for small producers. Unofficially: your antidote station."

"The committee didn't argue?" Adriano asked.

"They tried," Lorenzo said. "But I showed them pictures of my food. They became very cooperative."

Silvia rolled her eyes. "You also implied we might get a write-up from a certain international magazine if the event 'highlighted responsible food practices.'"

Cassidy blinked. "I did not agree to that."

"Well, you didn't *disagree* either," Lorenzo said. "And you have written for them before."

"Once," she said. "years ago."

"Semantics," he replied.

Enrico clapped his hands. "All right," he said. "We have machines. We have a recipe. We have a location. Now we need lemons. Sugar. Ice. People who can scoop without flirting."

Lorenzo put a hand on his chest. "Why are you looking at me?"

"Because you flirt with everyone," Enrico said. "We need speed, not seduction."

"I can multitask," Lorenzo protested.

Silvia cut in. "Focus," she said. "If we want enough granita for the first night, we have to start juicing. Now."

133

Cassidy grabbed a crate of lemons and a knife. Adriano took another. Elena set up a station to mix the drizzle into concentrated syrup they could then dilute batch by batch.

They worked as the afternoon stretched—cut, squeeze, strain, stir. Juice ran over their wrists, sticky and tart. Occasionally, someone would drift to the festival map to mark another detail, then come back to the lemons.

At one point, Nonna Vivi popped up on Silvia's phone screen, propped against the windowsill.

"You look tired," she announced immediately. "That means you're doing something important. Good."

"We're making granita," Silvia said.

"For the festival," Lorenzo added. "With a secret twist."

Nonna narrowed her eyes. "Is the twist murder?" she demanded.

"No," Cassidy said quickly. "Counter-murder."

"Bah," Nonna said. "Too many people try to kill with food. Not enough try to heal." She sniffed. "If I were there, this would already be over."

"If you were here," Giacomo's voice said faintly from off-screen, "the police would also be here."

"Police are decorative," Nonna said. "Real justice happens in kitchens."

Elena chuckled. "I like her," she said.

"Of course you do," Cassidy muttered. "My life is just a series of terrifying women feeding people justice."

"Could be worse," Adriano said. "They could be bad cooks."

Lines in the Sand

As the sun dipped, painting the hills in long shadows and gold, they finally stepped back from the chaos.

Two of the granita machines were already churning test batches, their transparent barrels slowly filling with pale, slushy lemon. Buckets of infused syrup cooled in the corner, lids labeled with

134

ratios and warnings. The generator had been tested and blessed. The freezers hummed.

They stood outside for a moment, at the edge of the yard, hands sticky, clothes splattered, looking at the sky.

"Tomorrow," Cassidy said, "we stand in that piazza and pretend this is just another food festival."

"Tomorrow," Adriano said, "we stand in that piazza and make sure it doesn't turn into a massacre."

"And after tomorrow?" Lorenzo asked.

"After tomorrow," Elena said, "Davide will either be on the back foot... or very, very angry."

"He's already angry," Silvia said. "This will make him sloppy."

Cassidy felt the weight of all of it pressing at her ribs—the farmer's shaking hands steadying, Marco's empty apartment, the crate at their gate, the missing stone at Santa Lucia, her mother's absence pulsing under every step.

She took a breath.

"This is our line," she said. "We can't stop the whole network in one night. We can't un-poison every jar or save everyone who's eaten from them. But this festival? This is a place we can draw a line. Here, now, he doesn't get to hide. Not behind pretty labels. Not behind discounts. Not in my town. Not with my people."

"Spoken like a Keeper," Elena murmured.

Cassidy grimaced. "Please don't," she said. "I'm barely keeping myself."

"You're doing more than that," Adriano said quietly.

Silence settled, softer this time.

Then Lorenzo's phone buzzed.

He frowned at the screen. "Unknown number," he said.

Cassidy's stomach clenched. "Don't answer," she said.

"So we just let it ring?" he asked.

"It's probably spam," Silvia said. "Or Davide. Which is also spam."

The phone stopped. Started again. Same number.

135

On the third ring, Elena stepped forward and plucked it out of Lorenzo's hand.

"I'll answer," she said. "If it's him, he's not expecting my voice."

Before anyone could argue, she tapped the screen and lifted it to her ear.

"Pronto," she said.

There was a brief crackle. Then a voice.

Male. Calm. Too calm.

"Signora Valenti," it said. "How nice to hear you're still... involved."

Cassidy felt her blood go cold.

Elena's expression didn't change. "You have me at a disadvantage," she said. "Who is this?"

"You know," the man said. "Even if you pretend you don't. I enjoyed your dinner at Santa Lucia."

Davide.

Not cheap-suit messenger boy. The man himself.

Cassidy's breath stuttered. Adriano moved closer to Elena, as if proximity could alter a phone call.

"You have interesting timing," Elena said. "We were just talking about you."

"I hope it was flattering," Davide said. "I do so enjoy being the center of attention."

"It was more... technical," she said. "Side effects. Casualties. You know how it is."

He chuckled. "Still sharp," he said. "Your friend Catherine always said you were the only one who could keep up with her in the kitchen and in the argument."

"Catherine is dead," Elena said. "And you helped."

A pause.

"I warned her," Davide said. "You can't change a system from the outside. Not at scale. You have to own it. I offered her a chair at the table. She preferred to throw rocks through the window."

136

"She preferred not to kill people for market share," Elena snapped.

"Collateral," he said. "Damage. There's always some. You of all people know that. How many chickens died for your ethics?"

"Not the same," she said through her teeth.

Cassidy wanted to rip the phone out of her hand and scream, but she stayed very, very still.

"What do you want?" Elena asked. "Besides to hear yourself talk."

"I want to offer you all a chance to survive this with minimal... inconvenience," he said. "Call it professional courtesy. For old times' sake."

"We're not interested," she said.

"You haven't heard the terms," he replied. "They're very generous. You stop whatever little... project you're running. You don't show up at the festival. You don't meddle with my brand. In return, I don't escalate."

"Escalate how?" Elena asked, even though they all knew.

"You've already lost one mother," he said, his tone flattening. "It would be a shame to lose a grandmother too."

Every muscle in Cassidy's body locked.

Nonna.

Bocce and Nina and Brunella's terrifying cousin-house. Supposedly safe because who would be insane enough to poke that nest.

"You don't know where she is," Elena said, but there was a thread in her voice now that wasn't quite steady.

"I know where she isn't," Davide said. "She's not as invisible as you think, Elena. None of you are. I've been polite. I sent messages. Crates. Bullets that missed. A boy from a gelato shop who may or may not find his way home." A beat. "I don't enjoy this part. But I will do it. Because someone has to decide whose sweetness is worth preserving."

"You're insane," Elena said softly.

137

"No," he replied. "I'm pragmatic. The festival will happen. The honey will flow. The gelato will melt in happy mouths. You can either stand aside and let the market run its course, or you can throw yourselves under the wheels and be crushed." Another pause. "You have until tomorrow morning to decide. I'll call again. If I don't like your answer… I start looking for old women who like bocce."

The line went dead.

For a long, brittle second, no one moved.

Then Cassidy exploded.

"Son of a—" She cut herself off, hands curling into fists, vision prickling. "He does not get to say her name. He does not get to threaten her. He does not—"

Adriano caught her shoulders. "Hey," he said. "Breathe."

She did, once, twice, so hard it hurt.

"We can move her," Silvia said, voice sharp with adrenaline. "Brunella's is safe but not invincible. Giacomo can take her deeper into the hills, somewhere with fewer neighbors and more shotguns."

"We can't guarantee that," Lorenzo said. "Every move we make, he sees more."

"We don't have to move her," Elena said slowly, eyes distant. "We have to make it so he can't afford to touch her."

"How?" Cassidy demanded. "He clearly thinks he can afford anything."

"We make the cost higher than the benefit," Elena said. "We make it so visible, so loud, that if he lays a finger on someone's grandmother, the narrative shifts. He stops being a clever, invisible supplier and becomes a cartoon villain. Investors don't like cartoon villains. Neither do judges. He's arrogant, not stupid. He knows there's a point where the story turns on him."

"And you think we can push him there?" Adriano asked.

"With the right proof, the right witnesses, the right timing?" Elena said. "Yes. The festival gives us that. Thousands of people.

138

Cameras everywhere. Journalists. Livestreams. If we can catch him in the act—his product making people sick while ours helps them —we don't just save lives. We weaponize outrage."

Cassidy wiped her face roughly. She hadn't realized she was crying until her sleeve came away damp.

"So we don't back down," she said, voice low and fierce. "We go harder."

"We also call Giacomo," Silvia said. "Now. Nonna moves tonight. Quietly."

"I'll handle it," Lorenzo said, already pulling out his phone.

Enrico looked at the sky, fists on his hips. "He made his line," he said. "Now we make ours."

Cassidy thought of chapter arcs again. Of all the stories she'd read and loved, the ones where the heroes faced an offer: step back and survive small, or step forward and risk everything.

She'd always rolled her eyes at how easily they chose "risk everything."

Now, standing in the fading light with lemon on her skin and fury in her chest, she understood.

"You don't get to decide who is worth saving," she whispered, as if Davide could somehow hear her across distance and plastic. "Not anymore. Not here. Not now."

Adriano's hand found hers again, warm and solid.

"Tomorrow night," he said. "Piazza. Granita. Antibiotics in citrus clothing. Cameras. Chaos."

"And Nonna," Cassidy said, swallowing. "Safe. Far away from his reach."

"And Marco," Lorenzo added quietly, snapping his phone shut. "Wherever they've taken him, he'll know someone's fighting back. Even if he never sees it."

The hill wind picked up, carrying the scent of grapes and distant woodsmoke. The machines hummed behind them, steadily freezing sugar and lemon into something that might pass for hope.

The part where the villain stops hinting and starts threatening openly.
The part where you either flinch... or you sharpen the knife.
"We sharpen," she said.
No one argued.

Chapter 8 – The Woman in White and the House of Glass

The next morning broke with a cold clarity that felt like God himself was leaning down to tell them:
Tonight decides everything.
The granita vats churned in the courtyard like slow, patient beasts.
The infused drizzle cooled in labeled jars.
Freezers hummed with focused purpose.
And Cassidy hadn't slept.
Not really.
She'd drifted in and out while moonlight crept across the ceiling and Adriano's arm lay heavy across her waist.
For hours she stared into the dark, thinking of Nonna Vivi, of Marco, of her mother, of Catherine's ledger—the map of a war her mother never lived to finish.
By dawn, one thought rang clear:

Someone bigger than Davide had to be pulling these strings.

Davide was cruel.
He was cunning.
But he wasn't a visionary.
Someone else was building something vast.
Someone else had the money, the reach, the ambition.
Someone else wanted towns like Montaione to wither.
That someone had just stepped out of the shadows.

The Letter in the Crate

At seven a.m., as fog hugged the vineyard rows, Silvia discovered the crate propped against the gate.
Wooden.
New.

Expensive.
Like the one at the convent.
Like the one in Siena.
Cassidy sprinted down the path as Silvia pried it open with a crowbar.
Inside was not a threat.
Not a weapon.
A letter.
Hand-written on cream stationery so thick it could've doubled as armor.
Lorenzo read aloud, voice low and steady:

"To the Keepers—
You have interfered.
Not disastrously.
Not yet.
But your persistence has become inconvenient.
So before tonight's festivities, I felt compelled to clarify the stakes.
I purchased your town years ago.
I simply haven't collected it yet.
–B.M."

Lorenzo flipped the card over.
It was embossed:

BIANCA MORETTI
TerraNova Group
Future Built Forward™

Cassidy's knees nearly buckled.
Bianca Moretti.
Not just rich.
Infamous.

The tech visionary who sold "GlobeMind," the first predictive crisis-management AI, for 6.2 billion dollars and then vanished into "ethical agritech philanthropy."

Real estate.

Autonomous vineyards.

"Regenerative village clusters."

The news articles came flooding back.

Cassidy had skimmed them the year before moving to Italy. And now—

now the dots connected like a lightning bolt.

The poisoned honey.

The shrinking towns.

The sick farmers.

The abandoned houses.

The missing stone at Santa Lucia—the stone marked with her mother's symbol.

The distribution map that looked like a neural network.

Bianca wasn't trying to destroy Tuscany.

She was terraforming it.

Cassidy stepped back, breath catching. "She ... wants the land."

"Not just wants," Elena murmured. "She's acquiring it."

"Why poison people?" Silvia demanded. "Why make them sick?"

"Because sickness makes people break," Adriano said quietly. "Break their shops. Break their families. Break their generational attachments. When your body betrays you, you start looking for help. For security. For buyouts."

"And who swoops in?" Lorenzo said. "The woman with capital."

"TerraNova," Cassidy whispered. "Future Built Forward."

Elena rubbed her temples. "Catherine suspected someone was orchestrating market collapse. She thought it was corporate sabotage at first. Then she found traces—financial patterns—that led to someone private. A benefactor with no obvious motive. She was close."

Cassidy swallowed. Her mother hadn't just been fighting poison.

She had been fighting a hostile takeover of rural Italy.

The Meeting at the Glass House

The second envelope in the crate held coordinates.

A location ten minutes outside Montaione.

A time: *2:00 p.m.*

An invitation—or a summons.

"We go," Adriano said immediately.

"No," Elena interjected sharply. "This is a trap."

"She wants to talk," Cassidy said. "She wants us to stand down. If she wanted us dead, she wouldn't have written a letter. She would've sent a bullet."

"She already sent bullets," Silvia reminded them.

"But not at us," Cassidy countered. "Not directly. She still thinks she can negotiate."

Lorenzo crossed his arms. "So we go. But not alone."

Cassidy took a breath.

"I'll go," she said. "She's addressing the Keepers. That's me. She knows it's me."

"You're not going alone," Adriano said sharply.

"I'm not leaving you behind," she replied.

Elena looked up from the letter. "Three of us," she decided. "Cassidy, Adriano, Lorenzo. Too many and she'll feel ambushed. Too few and she'll feel superior."

Enrico grunted. "I will hide in the trunk."

"You are absolutely not hiding in the trunk," Silvia said.

"I can be very quiet," he insisted.

"No."

A Drive Like No Other

The sun climbed.

The air warmed.

The festival sounds began to rise from the distant piazza—testing microphones, carts rolling into place, children shouting.

But none of it touched the car as it wound through the hills, gravel popping beneath the tires.

Cassidy sat in the backseat, staring at the letter.

At the elegant handwriting.

At the confidence in every stroke.

Bianca Moretti had addressed her as "Keeper."

Her mother's mantle.

Her mother's fight.

"What if she knew Catherine?" Cassidy murmured.

Elena, at the wheel, didn't look away from the road. "She did."

Cassidy's head snapped up. "What?"

"They crossed paths twice," Elena said. "Both in academic circles. Catherine admired her brilliance. Bianca admired Catherine's ethics. They debated for hours. Always friendly, always civilized."

"What happened?"

Elena exhaled, long and low. "Catherine once told me that Bianca was the most dangerous mind she'd ever met. Because she didn't believe in borders—ethical or geographic. She believed in optimization. At any cost."

Cassidy's stomach tightened.

"What Catherine never figured out," Elena continued, "was whether Bianca was trying to save the world … or replace it."

"And now?" Adriano asked quietly.

Elena's knuckles tightened on the steering wheel. "Now I think she's tired of waiting."

The Villa of Glass and Steel

It appeared suddenly around a bend—a jarring, modern palace set in a sea of vines.

Glass walls.

Steel beams.

Sharp lines.

No shutters.

No clay tiles.

No history.

It was a monument to power standing defiantly in ancient soil.

Elena parked near a gravel path. "She built this two years ago," she said. "Locals protested. She claimed it was for wine innovation. It's a command center."

They walked the final stretch.

Cassidy felt her pulse thudding at the base of her skull.

The front doors glided open without being touched.

Motion sensors.

Heat mapping.

AI triggers.

Bianca Moretti hadn't left tech behind.

She'd embedded it in her empire.

Inside, the villa was… sterile.

White stone.

Polished concrete.

A living wall of moss under glass.

Shelves filled not with books but with awards.

A few pieces of art—abstract, angular, cold.

And at the center:

A woman in a white suit.

Tall.

Silver hair pulled into a knot.

Eyes sharp enough to cut silk.

A posture that radiated: *I built an empire, and now I'm building another.*

She turned as they entered.

"Ah," she said. "The Keepers arrive."

The Mastermind Speaks

Bianca Moretti smiled the way a surgeon smiles before making an incision.

"Cassidy Moore. Adriano Vitale. Lorenzo Bressani. I am delighted you accepted my invitation."

Cassidy felt every muscle tighten. "You made it sound compulsory."

"Most truth is," Bianca replied. "Especially the kind that reshapes the world."

She gestured to a sleek table. Four chairs.

She sat.

They didn't.

"Tea?" she offered. "Water? Basil lemonade? It's quite refreshing."

"No," Adriano said.

Bianca nodded, unfazed. "Straight to business. Very well."

Her gaze sharpened.

"You've made my work... inconvenient."

"We're stopping your work," Lorenzo said.

Bianca folded her hands. "My dear boy. My work is progress."

Cassidy stepped forward. "Your work is poisoning people."

"No," Bianca corrected. "My work is accelerating inevitability."

Elena exhaled sharply. "Here we go."

Bianca continued, serene.

"I adore Tuscany. Truly. But it is inefficient. Aging. Fragmented. These tiny towns, these fragile farms, these ancient homes held together with nostalgia and duct tape—none of them can compete with global markets. Not anymore."

Cassidy felt her jaw clench. "So you destroy them?"

"I free them," Bianca said. "I buy them. I integrate them. I repurpose them. I take land that is dying and make it productive again. Scalable. Connected. Beautiful."

"And the honey?" Adriano demanded. "The poison?"

Bianca's expression softened as if she were speaking to a child who'd misunderstood something obvious.

"People do not give up land when they are comfortable," she said. "They move when they feel unsafe. Uncertain. Vulnerable. Davide's little chemical agent created discomfort. Not death."

"You killed Giulia," Lorenzo snapped.

Bianca tilted her head. "Giulia was brilliant. But she interfered. She tried to expose Davide. She threatened the structure before it was stable."

"And my mother?" Cassidy whispered. "What about Catherine Moore?"

Bianca's eyes flicked to her, assessing, calculating.

"Catherine was extraordinary," she said softly. "She saw patterns most people miss. She saw what I was doing before it had begun. She warned me that I was 'playing god with ecosystems.' And I told her she was trying to stop a tsunami with a teaspoon."

Cassidy's voice cracked. "Did you kill her?"

Bianca did not look away.

"I did not touch her," she said. "But she refused to join me. She refused to stay silent. And she refused to disappear. The world has a way of correcting such imbalances."

Lorenzo made a sound like he was about to lunge across the table.

Bianca didn't flinch.

"Marco?" Adriano demanded. "Where is he?"

Bianca smiled faintly. "Your gelato boy is alive. Frightened, confused, slightly bruised. But alive."

"Where?" Cassidy pressed.

"He'll be released after the festival," Bianca said. "Assuming you cooperate."

Silence crashed into the room.

Cassidy's heartbeat rang in her ears like war drums.

Bianca steepled her fingers.

148

"I know what you're planning," she said. "The granita stand. The antidote disguised as lemon ice. Very clever. Catherine would be proud."

"Then you know we won't stop," Cassidy said.

Bianca nodded once. "I do. And so I am offering you one chance—just one—to walk away alive."

She stood.

"At six o'clock tonight, you will leave Montaione," she said. "You will drive to Florence. You will get on a plane tomorrow morning. And you will never come back."

"No," Adriano said immediately.

"Think carefully," Bianca said. "Your Nonna Vivi is very... reachable."

Cassidy felt ice crawl down her spine.

"You hurt her," she said, "and I will burn your empire to the ground."

Bianca's smile widened. "Good. Catherine said you had fire."

Cassidy stepped closer. "You know what I am? What the Keepers were?"

Bianca waved a dismissive hand. "Caretakers of tradition. Recipes. Ethics. Romanticists. Stories meant to be replaced."

Her voice went colder.

"This is the future, Cassidy. Algorithms forecast yield. Drones pollinate flowers. Soil monitors decide which farm lives and which dies. Italy must evolve or be sold for parts."

"You don't get to decide that," Cassidy said.

"Oh," Bianca whispered, leaning in. "But I already have."

The Final Warning

They turned to leave.

Bianca didn't stop them.

Didn't threaten them again.

Didn't raise her voice.

149

But just as they reached the glass doors, she said:
"Oh—one more thing."
They paused.
"If you insist on your little display tonight," she said lightly, "do keep your eyes open. Accidents happen at large events. Stoves explode. Generators fail. Crowds stampede."
Her gaze drifted to Cassidy.
"People disappear."
Cassidy didn't breathe.
Bianca Moretti smiled.
"Enjoy the festival."

A Painful Ride Back

The car was silent.
Utterly, painfully silent.
The hills flashed past.
The vines blurred.
The sky lowered.
Then Cassidy whispered, "She killed my mother."
Elena tightened her grip on the wheel. "Indirectly. But yes."
"She orchestrated all of it," Lorenzo said. "Giulia. The honey. The tunnels. The crates."
"And she has Marco," Adriano added.
No one spoke for a long stretch of road.
Finally, Cassidy lifted her head.
"She thinks she already owns this place," she said. "She thinks she can take it without a fight."
"She thinks she can take everything," Elena said.
Cassidy inhaled slowly. "Then tonight we don't just save the festival."
She met Adriano's eyes.
"We expose her."

150

Back at the Vineyard

Enrico listened to the entire story without interrupting.

When it finished, he spat on the ground. "A billionaire," he muttered. "Of course. Only the rich look at a beautiful thing and think, 'I want to break it so I can own the pieces.'"

Silvia paced. "We can't fight someone with her money. Her reach. Her lawyers."

"We don't need to fight her money," Lorenzo said. "We need to fight her story."

Cassidy pulled the crate's letter from her pocket. "She said she bought this town. She thinks the people here don't matter. That they'll fold."

"They won't," Adriano said.

"They will," Cassidy countered. "Unless they know the truth."

Elena looked up from her notes. "Then tonight is not about antidotes alone. It's about information. Witnesses. Evidence. We gather everything she confessed today. We gather every clue from the last three books. We tie it together. And we hand it to the world."

"And Marco?" Adriano asked.

"Bianca said he'll be released after the festival if we back down," Cassidy said. "Which means he's either on site ... or she plans to use him as leverage."

"We find him," Lorenzo said. "Before she decides he's no longer useful."

The Missing Stone Finally Speaks

Cassidy dug the stone fragment from her bag.

Catherine's symbol.

A Keeper's mark.

The missing piece from behind Santa Lucia's altar.

151

She pressed it to the table.

Elena leaned over, eyes widening. "Cassidy. Did you notice the carving on the back?"

"I didn't understand it," Cassidy said. "It looked like... a map."

"It is," Elena whispered. "It's coordinates. Latitude. Longitude."

"To what?" Adriano asked.

Elena picked up her phone, entered the numbers, and paled. "Oh God."

"What?" Cassidy demanded.

"The coordinates point to—"

Silence.

Then—

"A storage facility behind Bianca's villa."

A beat.

"And there's a second marker," Elena said slowly, tracing the symbol. "A smaller coordinate. Less precise. A circle with three lines."

Cassidy leaned in. "What does that mean?"

Lorenzo's breath caught.

"It's a trapdoor symbol," he whispered. "Old architectural shorthand used in monasteries and wine cellars."

Silvia frowned. "Trapdoor where?"

Elena tapped the symbol.

"Beneath Montaione's piazza."

Cassidy felt the world tilt.

Beneath the very place where thousands of people would gather tonight.

"That's why she chose the festival," she whispered. "That's why she needs crowds. She's staging something."

Adriano's voice dropped. "We need to cancel the event."

"We can't," Silvia said. "She'd leak it. Spin it. We'd look like saboteurs."

"Then what?" Lorenzo asked.

Cassidy straightened.

"We go," she said. "We stand at our stall. We serve antidote. We gather evidence. And while the festival moves around us…"

She tapped the trapdoor symbol.

"…we find what she hid beneath the piazza."

"What if it's empty?" Silvia asked.

"It won't be," Elena said. "Bianca never leaves anything to chance."

"And what if it's dangerous?" Lorenzo added.

Cassidy looked at each of them, one by one.

"It is dangerous," she said. "Everything has been dangerous. But we're closer than we've ever been. We know who the villain is. We know her plan. And tonight, we make sure the world knows too."

Adriano stepped beside her.

"I'm with you," he said simply.

Lorenzo nodded. "Always."

Silvia inhaled. "We're doing this. God help us."

Elena looked at the symbol one last time, then pocketed the stone. "Then let's finish what Catherine started."

Enrico cracked his knuckles. "And after we expose her, we make gelato. Because justice is best served frozen."

Cassidy laughed—a sharp, tired, emotional sound.

Then she squared her shoulders.

"Tonight," she said, "we end this."

And somewhere, in a clean, cold villa of glass and steel, Bianca Moretti checked her watch and smiled.

The game was set.

The festival lights were being strung across Montaione's streets.

The trapdoor waited beneath the piazza.

And every unresolved thread from the last three books was pulling tight—toward a single point of collision.

Tomorrow would be the finale.
Tonight would be the reckoning.

Chapter 9 – The Night the Sweetness Fought Back

By six o'clock, Montaione's piazza glowed like a lantern cupped in God's hands.

Strings of bulbs zigzagged between buildings. Vendors shouted over each other. Children ran in circles with sticky hands and wild abandon. Musicians played a frantic folk rhythm that was equal parts joyous and foreboding, like a celebration held on the edge of a cliff.

At the center of it all—Cassidy's granita stand.

A wooden booth draped in lemon-yellow linens, a banner that read:

SOLIDARITY GELATO / KEEPERS' DELIGHT (suggested donation: a smile)

Behind the counter, three granita machines hummed with purpose.

Freezers buzzed like docile beasts.

Cassidy stood between Adriano and Lorenzo, apron on, ladle ready, heart pounding like a war drum.

She scanned the crowd, looking for danger in every face.

"Remember," Elena said behind them. "Tonight's goal is threefold: distribute antidote safely, gather evidence, and find the trapdoor."

"And try not to die," Silvia added.

Enrico crossed himself dramatically. "And if you do die, make sure it's not on my granita machine. They are borrowed."

Cassidy attempted a breath. Failed.

"It's starting," Adriano whispered.

Oh yes.

It was starting.

The mayor marched onto the main stage, flanked by two assistants wearing elaborate sashes and the expression of people who'd rather be anywhere else.

He tapped the microphone.

"Welcome, citizens of Montaione!" he cried, arms wide. "Tonight we celebrate the sweetness of tradition, the purity of our past, and the bright future of—"

Something metallic clanged in the distance.

Cassidy jumped.

Silvia muttered, "Probably a spoon."

The mayor continued. "—our proud honey and gelato heritage! Let us feast, let us sing, and let us—"

On the far side of the piazza, a small crowd began coughing.

Hard.

Sharp.

Rhythmic.

Cassidy's breath stopped.

Adriano's hand found hers.

"Go," he murmured.

They pushed through the crowd, hearts thundering.

The First Collapse

A middle-aged man leaned against a brick wall, hand pressed to his chest. His breath came in uneven bursts. A woman beside him clutched her stomach, knees buckling.

Recognizable symptoms.

The ones Cassidy had learned to fear.

Metallic taste.

Racing pulse.

Sudden nausea.

Davide's poison.

Elena shoved through the crowd like a surgeon cutting through tissue. "Symptoms began how long ago?"

"Ten minutes," the woman gasped.

155

"Journalist from Siena," the man wheezed. "Ate... the honey gelato... at stall six."

Silvia cursed violently. "Davide's dosing festival stands. He's using the vendors."

Cassidy grabbed the emergency pouch of infused drizzle from her bag. "Give them this."

"But we haven't tested it on—" Elena began.

"Give it to them!" Cassidy snapped.

Elena didn't hesitate. She unscrewed the jar, scooped a portion, and fed it to the woman like communion. Then to the man.

They held their breath.

Ten seconds.

Fifteen.

Twenty.

The woman's breathing steadied first.

The man's pulse slowed. He blinked, chest loosening.

Cassidy nearly collapsed in relief.

"It works," Adriano whispered.

Silvia exhaled. "Then tonight... we save as many as we can."

And then—

A scream tore across the piazza.

The kind that silences a crowd instantly.

Cassidy spun—and froze.

The Trapdoor Opens

The center of the piazza—just in front of the ancient fountain—was shifting.

Stone tiles rattled.

The earth shuddered.

A circle of pavement sank an inch, then another.

A trapdoor.

Exactly where the stone symbol had indicated.

People stumbled backward. Some ran. Vendors shouted. A dog barked wildly.

Cassidy's heart slammed into her ribs.

"Lorenzo," she gasped. "It's right where the symbol pointed."

He nodded, jaw tight. "Bianca hid something underground."

"Or someone," Adriano said.

The trapdoor lurched again.

Then—

It opened.

A slow, mechanical rise.

Not rustic.

Not medieval.

Hydraulics.

A steel platform emerged from below.

And on that platform—

Sitting bound in a chair

Eyes wide—

was Marco.

Cassidy's breath left her.

"Marco!" Adriano shouted.

Marco's throat worked. "Get... away... from here..."

But before they could move, another figure appeared behind him.

A woman in a white suit.

Bianca Moretti.

She stepped onto the platform as if emerging onto a stage she'd built herself.

The crowd gasped.

No one recognized her—yet.

But Cassidy did.

Bianca leaned in toward Marco, one manicured hand resting on his shoulder in a gesture so intimate it was poisonous.

"Good evening, Montaione," she called, voice amplified through a hidden speaker.

"What have you done?" Cassidy shouted.

"Nothing," Bianca said sweetly. "Yet. But the night is young."

The platform rose another foot and locked into place, level with the piazza.

Bianca stepped forward.

The crowd parted instinctively, like animals sensing a predator.

"Let me explain what is about to happen," she said gently, as if addressing kindergarteners.

"You see—your town is on the verge of extinction. Economically. Culturally. Biologically."

Cassidy's rage surged.

"STOP." She shoved her way forward. "No one wants your help!"

"Oh, Cassidy," Bianca sighed. "You're not here to stop me. You're here to *perform* for me."

She gestured toward the granita stand.

"Your little antidote experiment," she said. "Cute. Admirable. A testament to Catherine's stubbornness."

Cassidy felt her stomach twist.

Bianca lifted a remote.

Clicked a button.

And every vendor stall sign flickered.

Then—

Screens rose from behind booths.

A large screen emerged from behind Bianca and a camera crew appeared.

The entire piazza was suddenly live-streaming.

Bianca smiled directly into a camera.

"Hello, world," she said. "You may want to sit down."

The Broadcast

Bianca's voice echoed through the piazza and, seconds later, through every smart phone in Italy.

"Welcome to the Montaione Festival of Sweetness," she said. "Brought to you by TerraNova Group."

Cassidy's blood froze.

158

Behind Bianca, the screens displayed:

TerraNova Group
Future Built Forward™

Bianca continued, graceful as a snake.
"Tonight, we reveal a truth that has been hidden for far too long. This town—once beautiful—has been dying. Slowly. Quietly. Like so many rural pockets of Italy."
The crowd murmured.
"This region is inefficient," Bianca said. "Economically unviable. Environmentally mismanaged. Tradition cannot save it. Nostalgia cannot save it. Only innovation can."
"WE DON'T NEED YOU!" someone shouted.
"Yes," Bianca said softly. "Yes, you do. And we at TerraNova Group have the solution for you."
A prerecorded video advertising the company started to play.
Cassidy stepped forward into frame.
"No," she said firmly. "What we need is the TRUTH."
And then—
Silvia hit the button on their granita stand's hidden projector.
A giant image splashed across the main screen behind Bianca's head.
A jar of Davide's honey.
Next to it: an infrared scan showing the chemical agent and the words "Don't eat the honey! It's poisoned!"
People in the crowds started screaming and panicking.
Bianca didn't flinch.
Enrico and Lorenzo ran with full cups of granita towards the screams.
"Ah," she said. "I see you found out my little secret."
Cassidy's voice trembled with fury. "YOU were the one who poisoned the supply chain."

"I corrected it," Bianca said. "A small dose of discomfort encourages relocation. Consolidation. Cooperation. People are easier to move when they're already trembling."

"You're a monster," Lorenzo snarled.

"I'm a futurist," Bianca said. "And this town is Phase Three."

The crowd erupted.

"What did you do to Marco?" Adriano shouted.

Bianca tilted her head. "Oh, nothing permanent. He was merely... misled. He thought he was helping improve supply lines. He assumed the Keepers were interfering for sport."

Cassidy's heart sank.

"Marco," Bianca said loudly, turning him toward the crowd. "Tell them. Tell them why you helped me."

Marco's lips parted.

But no sound came. Bianca reached over and grabbed his jaw to plant a large red kiss on his cheek

Eyes flickering, Cassidy understood.

"He's drugged," she whispered.

Bianca smiled. "Only slightly. Enough to keep him quiet. He's my pet. I just give him enough to keep him obedient."

Adriano lunged forward. "You psychopath—"

Bianca raised the remote.

"And now," she said, "I remove my final obstacle."

She pressed a button.

Marco disappeared within the earth, and deep beneath the piazza—

A second mechanical sound echoed upward.

The sound of another platform rising.

Cassidy's breath vanished.

No.

No, no, no—

The platform rose.

A figure lay on it.

160

Small.
Still.
Wrapped in a blanket.
Nonna.
"NO!" Adriano roared.
Cassidy's eyes flooded.
Nonna Vivi—unmoving—lay on a cold steel slab.
The piazza erupted into hysterical cries at the sight of the dead grandmother.
Bianca lifted a hand.
"Do not worry," she said calmly. "Nonna Vivi has simply… served her purpose."
Cassidy fell to her knees.
"No," she whispered. "No, no—she's not—no—"
Bianca faced the crowd.
"Tonight, you choose," she said. "You either join TerraNova in the future… or you remain relics of a dying past."
Behind her, screens flickered.
Drone footage showed abandoned towns.
Closed shops.
Empty vineyards.
All properties Bianca now owned, followed by generated images of engineered plans for the towns, and new infrastructure.
Cassidy's chest grew tight.
Bianca lifted the remote once more.
"Thank you, and goodnight, Montaione."
She clicked—
The screens burst into static.
Her microphone cut.
She blinked. "What—"
A new voice boomed over the speakers.
"HELLO, MORTALS!"
Everyone turned.
The screen lit up with—
Nonna Vivi.

Alive.

Very alive.

And very pissed.

Standing in Brunella's kitchen, holding a ladle like a weapon.

"Surpriiiise!" she shouted. "You thought you killed me? HA! Takes more than a billionaire witch and her bad hair to end this Nonna!"

The entire piazza started in disbelief, first looking at the body laying on the metal slab and then at the video. The similarity was uncanny.

The entire piazza exploded with cheering, crying, and horror.

Cassidy sobbed so hard her ribs hurt.

Bianca staggered backward. "What—how—"

A door burst open beside the stage.

Giacomo stormed out, wielding a rolling pin. "YOU TOOK THE WRONG GRANDMOTHER!"

Behind him—Brunella rose from from under the sheet where she'd been playing dead upon the platform.

And coming alongside her was Enrico's Nina.

Snarling.

Bianca stumbled.

Cassidy rose.

Fire in her veins.

"You lost," Cassidy said.

Bianca backed toward the edge of the stage.

"You think this ends me?" Bianca hissed. "You think taking over a livestream will stop TerraNova?"

Lorenzo stepped forward.

"No," he said. "But this will."

He held up Catherine's ledger.

Open to the page detailing TerraNova's shell companies, chemical transport schedules, offshore accounts—everything Catherine had discovered.

162

A final page Bianca never knew Catherine wrote because it had been written in invisible ink, and the heat of their potion creations had unveiled the truth.

Sylvia projected the image onto the screen.

The crowd went silent as truth poured out:

Bianca Moretti
Illicit acquisitions
Poison distribution network
Forced relocation operations
Corporate biological disruption plans

The piazza roared like an awakening beast.

Bianca paled.

"Security!" she snapped. "Shut this DOWN!"

But her guards didn't move.

Because Nina had them cornered.

Cassidy stepped closer.

"You don't get to rewrite this story," she said. "Not while any of us breathe."

Bianca turned to run—

Too late.

Brunella swung a cast-iron skillet.

CLANG!

Bianca Moretti crumpled.

"This is for making me burn my lasagna!" Brunella shouted.

And, the crowd erupted.

The Underground Revelation

While local authorities swarmed, while Bianca was dragged away, while Montaione shook with shock and liberation—Cassidy, Adriano, Lorenzo, Silvia, and Elena climbed down through the open trapdoor. A long, cold tunnel stretched ahead.

Catherine's symbol glowed faintly from etched paint on the wall.

At the end: Rows of crates labeled with TerraNova's seal. Maps. Data. Financial flows.

Proof of everything.

And—

Marco.

Alive. Much more conscious now.

Wobbly, but alive.

Cassidy threw her arms around him.

He clung to her. "I didn't know," he whispered. "I swear—I didn't know what she planned."

"I know," Cassidy breathed. "You're safe."

Behind them, Adriano and Lorenzo caught Marco in a crushing embrace.

"Don't ever disappear again," Adriano murmured.

Marco nodded. "Promise."

Elena took out a locket that had a symbol from the diary carved on the outside. She reverently passed it on to Cassidy saying "I think this is for you".

Inside: A note.

Cassidy—
Truth is not sweet.
Truth is necessary.
Finish what we began.
—Your mother

Cassidy pressed the note to her heart.

And she cried.

For her mother.

For Giulia.

For Marco.

For Nonna.

For everyone harmed.

But also—
for the beauty left to save.

Aftermath

By midnight, the festival was still going—louder now, freer.
People toasted.
Danced.
Shouted.
Embraced.
Bianca had been arrested.
Davide vanished, but his network was exposed. It was only a matter of time.
Federal authorities arrived.
The antidote had saved dozens.
News outlets swarmed.
Cameras rolled.
Cassidy's name trended across Italy.
The Keepers had returned. And red scarves seemed to emerge from out of the woodwork.
Cassidy stood at the edge of the piazza, watching lanterns float upward into the night sky like tiny souls released.
Adriano stepped beside her.
"You did it," he said softly, handing her a red pashmina.
"We did," she corrected.
He took her hand.
"Cassidy Moore," he said, voice low and reverent, "you are the bravest person I've ever known."
She leaned her head on his shoulder.
"What now?" she murmured.
"Now?" he said. "We rest."
"And after that?"
He smiled faintly.
"We rebuild."

Lorenzo joined them with three cups of untouched lemon granita. "To Catherine," he said.

"To Giulia," Silvia added.

"To Nonna Vivi," Elena said.

Cassidy raised her cup.

"To Montaione."

They clinked.

Drank. Danced. Laughed.

Brunella stood at a table filled with food dishing it up like she was a part of the neighborhood.

Lorenzo and Elena discussed combining their cooking classes into a network.

Enrico watched Silvia pet his Nina and looked clearly smitten.

Adriano leaned over and engulfed Cassidy's full lips with his own.

Above them, the sky glowed.

The Twist — Nonna Vivi's Return

"MOVE ASIDE! MOVE ASIDE! OLD WOMAN COMING THROUGH!"

Nonna Vivi barreled through the crowd like a Mediterranean hurricane with her red scarf flapping. Giacomo was there at her side protesting loudly carrying a gigantic pan of lasagna.

Cassidy raced to her.

"NONNA!" she cried.

Nonna wrapped her in a hug so strong Cassidy's ribs threatened mutiny.

"YOU THOUGHT I WAS DEAD? PFFT."

She kissed Cassidy's forehead.

"I am too stubborn to die."

Cassidy sobbed-laughed. "I thought—Bianca showed—it was Brunella"

"Bianca is a liar, a fraud, and her shoes are ugly," Nonna said. "I watched the livestream and screamed from the absurdity so hard Nina fainted."

Cassidy laughed so hard she nearly fell.

Lorenzo hugged and kissed his Nonna next. "Never scare us like that again."

"I make no promises!" Nonna declared. "Now someone give me wine!"

The Keepers of Tuscany

Later, long after the festival quieted, Cassidy and Adriano sat on a stone wall overlooking the vineyard. The moon glowed like a blessing.

Cassidy rested her head on Adriano's shoulder.

"We can go anywhere now," she whispered. "Start over anywhere."

He brushed his thumb across her knuckles.

"We stay," he said. He lightly touched the locket necklace that now rest below her collarbone.

She looked up. "Here?"

"With these people," he said. "With this land. With this fight. With you."

"We can get some bees, start a bakery, create our own brand of olive oil, get our own Nina." he joked.

She kissed him gently.

Then deeply.

The kind of kiss that tasted like triumph.

Like future.

Like home.

Something within her fluttered gently at the thought of that future.

Below them, the town of Montaione flickered with lantern light, alive again.

Above them, the night carried the echoes of all they'd saved.

All they'd survived.

All they'd yet to become.

And far in the distance—somewhere in a locked government van—Bianca Moretti screamed at someone to call her lawyers.

But even they wouldn't be able to stop what came next.

The Keepers had returned. A new generation was at the helm.

And Tuscany would never fall quietly again.

THE
OLIVE OIL
SEDUCTION

Richard Lucchesi

THE
BALSAMIC
BETRAYAL

Richard Lucchesi

THE
TRUFFLE
REVELATION

Richard Lucchesi

GUNSHOTS
and
GELATO

Richard Lucchesi

THE
MOZZARELLA
MARRIAGE

Richard Lucchesi

RICHARD LUCCHESI

UNDER THE TUSCAN BLUNDER

ONE BABY, TWO ITALIAN CITIZENSHIPS, AND THREE HOUSES

LA DOLCE BLUNDER

DOLCE VITA

Preview of

Under the Tuscan Blunder

By Richard Lucchesi

Chapter 5 - The Garden: Trash, Rice and Birds

Our garden in Italy is not huge. It runs the length of our building, is about ten meters deep towards the river, and is two tiered with a small upper part on the far side in front of Space 3. A waist high rock wall runs the length of the garden facing the river. Ivy grows up, over and through it. If there wasn't a wall at the edge of the cliff, the garden wouldn't be nearly as enjoyable.

The other side of the wall is a ten meter drop off straight down to the Lima river that runs by our home. Down there, I call it the swamp. It's muddy in some spots almost like quick sand, and bugs linger like bad perfume. It's so humid where we live that some roads never dry up, even after weeks without rain. But our little emerald green river looks *so* beautiful from above; that is, until you take a closer look. Trash around the river's edge is often left to rot, and there's no enforcement for people who litter.

One huge monster of a tree in front of the Cantina used to tower over everything else until one of the neighbors rallied everyone to cut it down. And good thing we removed it. It was ill as suspected, with a huge metal stake running up the center core of the tree trunk. The arborist almost ruined his chain saw attempting to chop up the stump.

My wife loves gardens. In order to cope with the stress of everything, it seemed like the perfect place for her to get some fresh air. Even if shared, it's nice to have easily accessible outdoor space. The wall makes the garden complete. It's quite a serene little space, but la dolce vita it is not.

Upon our first in person glimpse as a couple, we arrived to a very, very overgrown garden that nobody seemed to manage nor care about. It was massively overgrown, full of dead leaves, and seemed to be used for all the wrong reasons. Someone left *an entire kitchen cabinet set*, along with full length bathroom mirrors and doors on the patio in front of the Cantina window. Piles of trash had been left to die in front of Space 3. Apparently, nobody had lifted a finger in the garden for years.

Trash is Complicated

Garbage must get Italians' blood pumping, because it's everywhere. Weekly in our little town, workers replace heavy duty black plastic bags in trash cans all over, but it's not enough. The collective community trashes the streets anyway. In parts of the south, trash piles up in public places so high with no where to go, and no end in sight. Some of it resembles a third world country.

Regular trash is picked up every Saturday morning in front of our home. If we want them to take it, and we do, we must use a special colored bag for Saturday's pickup. If it's not sorted properly, the collectors do not take it. Rejection materializes in the form of a large sticker stuck to your bag or bin notifying you of your mistakes. Even with regular trash pickup for everyone, the public bins down the street between our home and Bar Italia are constantly overflowing. There's trash all over the sidewalks and street, and that's just in front of our house. Everywhere you walk in Italy you see it.

Additionally, recycling in Tuscany is a six-day-a-week effort. Sundays and Wednesday are for food waste, Monday's are for glass, Tuesday is plastic, and Thursday is paper and cardboard. Each household has a different colored bin for each day, so households easily store five bins apiece. Bins get messy, sticky, and smelly quickly. We store our bins in the outside laundry room, but most others who live in buildings are not so fortunate. And just like on Saturdays, if recycling is not correctly sorted, it's rejected, *and* they reject often. Personally, I've had every day rejected at least once. Luckily, everyone has Saturdays off!

Is your head spinning yet? Remember: you need hard core recycling skills if you want any chance any at la dolce vita.

Truthfully, the trash system in Tuscany is one of the most complicated parts about living here. You and most others sort every day, and yet trash is all over the streets. It doesn't make sense. Occasionally, I miss America dearly when I'm in our laundry room sorting trash and recyclables several times throughout the day.

In the garden, it took lots of maneuvering, tons of trips to the recycling center outside town with carloads of trash, and many months of effort to reverse years of neglect. The majority of trash wasn't mine, either. In the process, I'd determine the cumbersome steps to schedule a bulk pick-up. A second electric weed-wacker would replace the first one that busted, and a battery-powered reciprocating saw would be purchased too. After all, we were the only ones cleaning up the garden, and trimming anything. Eventually, we'd tame the dragon collecting and growing out there, but would the endeavor be worth it? Would we discover la dolce vita at the end of the garden tunnel?

The Rice Conundrum

My pregnant wife and I had been living in Italy for less than a week when we saw our first neighbor. We were hanging out in the garden stepping on crunchy leaves, and casually removing overgrowth when we looked up and saw a woman with her daughter. They were watching us from a window above our main apartment. The woman was maybe in her early thirties with long, dark hair. Her daughter was about five years old. They seemed nice. We smiled and waved. The woman waved back, and then must have told her daughter to wave too. We'd stop cordially waving to each other soon enough.

The following morning something strange happened. At the bottom of the outside stairs into the garden was a big pile of uncooked white rice. It was scattered everywhere. Grains of rice were on the concrete stoop where we walk, in the grass, in a garden bed, and even stuck in leaves of nearby bushes. The rice must had fallen from a window. Had the same neighbor accidentally dropped rice out of the window?

I looked straight up. A small bag of food waste hung from a hook right below the woman's window. There's an apartment above hers, the top floor, but I had yet to witness any activity. The green shutters from the top apartment hadn't moved once. Whether inadvertently of otherwise, the rice must have come from the young woman's apartment directly above us. All activity above seemed to come from there.

I let it be. It could have easily been swept up, but it wasn't mine. Whoever did this would take care of it I figured. Seemed logical.

Apparently, this is *not* how la dolce vita works in Italy.

Two days go by, and nobody cleaned the rice. Being *very* new to the environment, I didn't want to assume anything. I also try extra hard to be kind to neighbors, especially in the beginning. But after two days, the rice was bothering me.

On day three, while outside in the garden, I noticed activity in the window above. I look up, and the young woman was opening a window. I waved, smiled, and she waved back. This was our second encounter.

"Excuse me. This white rice, is this yours?" I tried to ask politely in Italian, pointing at the concrete.

She either *didn't* understand, or *pretended* not to. A moment goes by, and nothing.

"White rice. Right here. Is this yours?" I reiterated.

"No," I heard her say, wagging her finger at me.

Her eyes widened like golf balls. The intonation on the word 'no' went up like a slide whistle. I'd never heard anyone say no like that before in Italian, and haven't heard it since. I looked back down at the rice, and the window slammed.

Had I just caught the neighbor in a lie? I took a deep breath, walked over to the shed, grabbed the broom and dustpan, and swept up the rice.

I wonder if she watched.

Patricia the Bird Lady

Another day, I spot an older lady in the garden from the terrace. She was standing at the rock wall facing the river. There was a small bag to her right, a plastic tray to her left, and you wouldn't believe what she was doing!

In the months leading up to the birth of our son, I was so eager to practice Italian language. I moved to Italy hoping to make new friends, speak Italian everyday, and quickly become fluent. I was ultra motivated. My Italian language classes were helping, but I hoped to chat with local people organically too. It wasn't difficult to strike up conversations with locals down at the bar per se. The much bigger challenge was establishing genuine connections.

I moseyed down the stairs and over to the neighbor to politely say hello in Italian. Patricia, as it turns out, is from Sardinia. To her left sat a pile of small, dead black feathered birds in the tray. She was holding one of the birds, plucking its feathers, and dropping them over the wall. On the right were several featherless birds in a plastic bag. I looked down, and black feathers collected amongst the ivy vines.

"My brother raises these black birds on his farm. He gives me the extras this time of year," I think is what she said.

She continued to pluck. I watched her technique. She held the bird in her left hand while plucking with her right. With each pull, a few feathers came out. It was a tedious process. It was like watching a child discover a new task for the first time. If she had done this before, it certainly didn't seem like it.

Patricia was elderly, and spoke with a heavy lisp. Between the lisp and her Sardinian accent, I couldn't understand everything she said. Still, I smiled and nodded like everything I was seeing and hearing was normal.

"These taste great when baked in the oven. Do you want some? I have too many. Go ahead. Take these ones here," Patricia urged.

Before I could say anything, Patricia pulled out a second tray from below the first one, and started piling birds onto it. Two.. three… four…..

"Here, take one more," she said, and set another bird on top of the four.

Jesus! What the fuck is going on *here*?

"No, no, no," I said, waving my hand to object while holding a smile together.

My body language might have insinuated to Patricia that I welcomed taking the birds. She either misread my interest, didn't notice, or didn't care. She might have prepared birds like this for dinner often, but I hadn't. However, it was already too late. Patricia insisted, handing the tray of dead birds over like she was gifting me something valuable.

"Wow! Grazie mille," I said, looking down at the tray.

Pina briefly explained how to prepare them, but I could no longer understand her. My ears had shut down. I didn't know whether to smile or barf.

I carried the tray up the stairs. Stephanie was resting on the couch.

"I met one of our neighbors in the garden, and you'll *never guess* what she just gave me," I said sarcastically, hiding the tray behind my back.

GRANDMA BACKPACKS ITALY

RICHARD LUCCHESI

Preview of

Grandma Backpacks Italy

By Richard Lucchesi

Chapter 7 – Seeing Assisi with My Eyes

After Pompeii, we took the train north to Salerno and checked into a small guesthouse tucked off a quiet street. The owner's son greeted us and gave a polite, rapid-fire tour of the apartment—two bedrooms, decent Wi-Fi, and a kitchen with questionable charm.

Before arrival, though, we'd had a full-blown communication breakdown. I'd tried calling and texting all afternoon—zero response.

"This is the number listed on the booking site," I said, setting my phone on the kitchen table. "I've texted, I've called, I even tried WhatsApp."

The young man leaned over to see for himself.

"Ah," he said, sighing. "We stopped using this number more than a year ago."

I blinked. "A year?"

"Yes. Maybe more."

"You might want to update that. Just in case, you know, anyone ever tries to contact you ever again."

He smiled sheepishly. "We'll change it."

He left. We collapsed. Grandma claimed her own room off the kitchen and parked herself on the small bed. Charlie immediately began racing in and out of her room with his Matchbox cars like it was the Daytona 500.

We rested our legs and caught up on emails, messages, and any remaining shreds of sanity. We didn't plan to stay long in Salerno —just a one-night stopover before pushing deeper into central Italy. But we were determined to make the most of it.

Guitar Strings and Spaghetti

By 9 p.m., hunger won. We headed out for dinner, weaving through slick, rain-soaked alleys under one undersized umbrella. The stone streets shimmered. Men with armfuls of umbrellas tried to upsell us every ten feet.

"La Traversa?" I asked, checking my phone.

Stephanie nodded. "That's the one. Reviews said a guy plays guitar outside."

As we approached, there he was. Mid-strum. Singing gently under the awning, his voice just soft enough to feel like part of the atmosphere. Charlie spotted him first and broke into a sprint, his little feet splashing through puddles. I reached into my pocket, pulled out some coins, and handed them to Charlie.

"Go ahead, buddy. Give them to the man."

Charlie took them without hesitation, marched over, and dropped them into the small bucket at the guitarist's feet.

The man stopped strumming just long enough to smile wide and say, "Grazie, piccolo."

Inside, we were led up a narrow spiral staircase to a lofted seating area. Just three tables. We were alone up there, overlooking the kitchen like food critics with insider access. We ordered wine —red and sparkling—and a round of comfort food: spaghetti for Stephanie and Charlie, sausage and vegetables for Grandma, and meatballs for me. Charlie slurped noodles like he feared someone might steal the plate at any moment. The food was phenomenal.

Midway through the meal, the guitarist came inside. He began singing a gentle, Italian rendition of "Stand By Me." I didn't understand every word, but I didn't need to. It was perfect.

I tipped him again on the way out. He nodded graciously. We were all floating.

The Sliding Door of Doom

Back at the guesthouse, disaster returned. A loud *thwack* echoed through the kitchen.

I jumped. "You okay?!"

Grandma stood in the doorway to her room, wincing.

"I'm fine. This door is weird," she muttered.

She wasn't wrong.

185

Her "room" was more like a repurposed broom closet. The bed sagged. The space wasn't large. And the sliding door—which should've offered privacy—had been *wired shut* at the top with what looked like coat hangers and regret.

"Are you sure?" I asked, inspecting her foot.

She nodded. "Just bumped it."

I kneeled and gently touched her knee.

"That's a pretty big red mark."

"It's fine," she said. "I'm a tough chickadee."

Just then, Charlie burst into the room like he'd been shot out of a cannon.

"There's my little handsome guy!" Grandma said, grinning.

"Gran-ma! Gran-ma!" he shouted, climbing onto the bed.

"Charlie, give Grandma a big hug!"

She opened her arms. He dove in. I stood back, arms crossed, watching something beautiful unfold. It was a fleeting moment, one of those little sparks that feels eternal. Another apartment, another city, another one-night memory already slipping into the folds of nostalgia.

Mocha Pot Massacre

I woke around five to a *thud*. It sounded like something heavy had fallen nearby.

This is not unusual in Italy, where walls are shared and gravity is dramatic. I chalked it up to a neighbor's shelf collapsing and went back to sleep. At seven, I showered. The mattress we'd slept on had all the ergonomic support of a canoe, but whatever— espresso was coming.

By 8:30, I was in the kitchen brewing coffee. Grandma was sitting quietly in the living room. Stephanie and Charlie were still asleep. I found a mocha pot in the cabinet—one of *six*. The gasket felt a little wobbly, but I adjusted it, filled the water, spooned in the grounds, and lit the gas.

186

The scent began rising. I turned my attention to the breakfast nook.

Suddenly—**BOOM**.

It was a sharp *crack*, like a firecracker in a closed room. I spun around. The mocha pot had exploded.

Espresso covered everything—the walls, the backsplash, the stove, the counter, two chairs, the white tablecloth, the *refrigerator*. I stood there blinking, brown droplets dripping from my arm.

"Damn it!" I shouted.

"What happened?!" Stephanie yelled from the bedroom.

Grandma appeared in the doorway. "Are you okay?"

"I think the gasket blew out. This thing's been used way too many times."

"I'll help you clean," Stephanie said, appearing in the doorway. Grandma was already moving. Veteran instincts.

"This is ridiculous," I muttered. "There are five other pots in the cabinet. Why keep the one that's about to join a war crimes tribunal?"

We scrubbed for thirty minutes. Most of the stains came out. The rest would need an exorcism or a washing machine.

I selected a *different* mocha pot, one that looked like it had fewer emotional issues, and brewed another round.

This one held.

We finally sat down with our coffee. The kitchen was almost clean again. But our nerves? Less so.

She Fell and Didn't Tell

On the train to Perugia, I turned to Grandma.

"How'd you sleep?"

She shrugged. "Fine."

There was a pause.

"Actually... I fell last night."

"What?!"

187

"In the bathroom. The floor was uneven. I slipped, fell on my hip. But I'm fine!"

I stared at her. "You're not serious, are you?" I asked, sincerely.

"I didn't want to make a fuss."

She smiled and took a sip of water.

"You *fell* and didn't tell me?"

"I told you now," she said, grinning.

Stephanie and I looked at each other, stunned.

"You're unbelievable," I said.

"I'm a tough chickadee," she said again, looking proud.

The train rocked gently, countryside sliding past in green and gold. I stared at her for a moment, trying to decide whether to be angry, impressed, or both. She just smiled. Calm. Composed. Like slipping in a centuries-old bathroom at midnight was simply part of the itinerary.

I leaned back in my seat, shook my head, and exhaled. She really was a tough chickadee.

And as much as it terrified me sometimes, I had to admit—there was something unshakably comforting about that.

Even now.

Especially now.

A Holy Glimpse

Something incredible happened on the way to Perugia. We were on the train, gliding through the hills of Umbria. I wasn't looking for anything. Just staring out the window, letting my brain unravel. Then—Grandma gasped.

"Is that... *Assisi?*"

I turned.

There it was.

Assisi rose in the distance like a floating dream—sitting perfectly on the hillside in a sort of triangle shape, its warm-colored buildings stacked in harmony with the mountain. Even from a distance, it radiated something. Grace. Stillness. Truth.

"It is," I said, quietly.

Grandma stared out the window. She didn't take her eyes off it. "It's beautiful," she whispered.

She pressed her hand to the window.

"I've always wanted to see Assisi," she continued. "It's St. Francis's city."

After it was out of sight, she told me about Father Jim Callan, a beloved priest from our hometown of Rochester, New York. He was passionate, progressive, and deeply tied to the values of St. Francis—humility, peace, compassion for the poor.

"He always wanted people to live like Francis," Grandma said. "To really live simply. Lovingly."

Less than two weeks later, just a few days after Grandma returned home, Father Callan passed away from cancer complications. It was surreal.

Somehow—without knowing—Grandma got to lay eyes on the city of St. Francis just days before losing one of the people who embodied him best. Life has a way of slipping sacred moments into the margins if you're paying attention.

We didn't plan to see Assisi. Didn't expect it. Didn't even know it was on our route.

But there it was.

And it saw us back.

GRANDMA
BACKPACKS
SICILY

RICHARD LUCCHESI

Preview of
Grandma Backpacks Sicily

By Richard Lucchesi

Chapter 3 – Uncanny Mafia Efficiency

We left the bar on a high. Between the warm welcome, the cappuccino artistry, and Charlie's first babyccino, we'd basically been adopted by the staff. It's hard to leave a place where you feel like family, but Sicily was waiting.

Calabria is a labyrinth. It reminded me of North Jersey — roads looping, branching, splitting into random exits only locals understand. Reggio Calabria's infrastructure was... well, let's just say "charming" in the same way a crumbling castle is charming.

"Why are we going this way?" Grandma asked as we zigzagged through narrow side streets.

"Because this way leads out of town without us driving into a wedding procession or down a dead-end alley," I said.

"Oh. Good plan," she said, gripping the seat in front of her like we were in a rally car.

Once we escaped the old-town maze and found the highway north, I could breathe easier. The road twisted along the edge of the Strait of Messina, the view of Sicily shimmering in the distance. Every kilometer or so, a speed camera reminded me that Italy's Big Brother doesn't sleep.

The Bartender Saved Us

The waitress's directions had been spot-on. Down the winding highway and under bridges we went. And then — like magic — we found our exit, and the harbor unfolded in front of us. The closer we got, the more workers in neon vests appeared, waving batons like air-traffic controllers. They were all men, none looked thrilled to be there, and they moved us along with the kind of precision that screamed *This is run by the mafia.*

"I've never seen this many men working at the same time," Grandma muttered.

"Because they're not 'working,'" I whispered back. "They're orchestrating."

"You mean like...?" She raised an eyebrow.

I gave a non-committal shrug. "Let's just say it's... *efficient.*" And it really was. Compared to my last ferry experience across Lake Champlain—where we waited an hour to cross a lake narrower than some Costco parking lots—this was a well-oiled machine.

Cars rolled forward in tight rows between low concrete dividers. Tractor trailers idled patiently, buses disgorged passengers, and the whole thing moved like clockwork.

"How long do we wait?" Grandma asked.

"We're gonna see," I said.

Right then, a man approached, scanned the QR code on our ticket, nodded, and waved us on. That was it—no fuss, no paperwork. I half-expected him to slip us a biscotti and say "Welcome to Sicily" right then and there.

"That was incredibly quick. Sicily here we come!" Grandma announced excitedly.

The *Most* Efficient Part of Italy

The ferry sat ahead, painted white and gray, antennas bristling like a porcupine. We bumped up the ramp, parked in a snug spot behind another car, and climbed out. The metal deck radiated heat through my shoes.

We climbed two tight flights of stairs to the observation deck, squeezing past a family who looked like they'd packed for a six-month voyage.

Charlie darted out first. "I see the water!" he yelled.

"Don't fall in," Grandma said immediately, because Grandma.

The engine's low rumble vibrated up through the deck, and then we were moving. The wind was warm but fresh, curling around us in lazy gusts. Sicily loomed ahead, dry and sunburned under the high noon glare. It wasn't long before the coastline grew sharper, the hills more defined.

"This is it?" Grandma asked, squinting.

"That's Sicily," I said.

She nodded. "Looks... brown."

"It's summer," Stephanie said. "It'll be prettier up close."

"Hmm," Grandma replied in a tone that could mean anything from *I agree* to *I'm reserving judgment until I see gelato.*

We were about halfway across the strait by then, and the boat hummed steadily under our feet. The water below was deep blue and glinting like polished glass, and the coastline ahead kept growing, inch by inch.

Charlie pressed himself against the railing, his little fingers gripping the metal, eyes darting between the horizon and the gulls trailing us. Stephanie snapped a few photos of him, then turned the camera on Grandma, who posed like she was doing a campaign for "Senior Travel Weekly," one hand on the rail, the other shielding her eyes.

"Make sure you get my good side," she said.

"That's both sides," I called over the wind.

We all laughed, and then I pulled out my phone and started filming—panning from the ship's wake to the outline of Sicily, catching Grandma mid-suspicious glare at the crew below.

"You know," she said, leaning toward me, "I'm just saying... this whole thing runs too smoothly. All these men with matching batons? No women? No chaos? That's not normal. This is some *Godfather Part II* stuff."

"Grandma," I said, "it's called organization."

"It's called *connections*," she shot back, smirking. "Somebody's cousin is making a fortune."

"Just enjoy the ride," Stephanie said, laughing.

"I *am* enjoying it," Grandma replied. "I'm just saying... when things are this efficient in Italy, you should be suspicious."

I kept filming as she spoke, partly to capture the view and partly to record her commentary for future generations.

Before long, the brown slopes of Sicily began to show flecks of green, tiny white buildings appearing like scattered sugar cubes.

"Okay," Grandma said slowly, "I'll admit... it's starting to look less like Arizona and more like Italy now."

"Give it ten minutes," I said. "And maybe some bruschetta."

Her eyes lit up. "Now you're talking."

A Quick Tour of Messina

When we docked in Messina, the disembarkation was as organized as the boarding—lanes snaking between industrial buildings until we were spat out into the middle of the city. The streets were wider, cleaner, and somehow... calmer. Once we were away from the harbor, they were also very hilly.

And the waitress had been right—Sicily felt more put together. The roads were smooth, the signage clear, the traffic... reasonable.

Grandma leaned forward between the seats. "You know, I think I like it here already."

"You've been here for four minutes," Stephanie pointed out.

"Plenty of time to judge," Grandma said.

Messina immediately felt different from Reggio Calabria. The streets were broad, lanes clearly marked, and traffic actually obeyed the signals. Even the bus stops were neatly arranged—tall glass shelters with clean benches and posted timetables. An orange-and-white *ATM Messina* city bus hissed to a stop in front of us, letting off a small crowd of commuters in business clothes. Another pulled in right behind it, this one bound for *Annunziata Alta*.

We rolled past a row of elegant, pale-yellow buildings with ornate balconies dripping with plants, wrought-iron railings curling like ribbon. A grand neoclassical structure—columns, marble steps, the works—stood just ahead, the kind of building that made you instinctively check your shirt for wrinkles.

"What's that?" Grandma asked.

"Courthouse, I think," I said.

"Looks expensive," she said. "Bet the bathrooms inside are marble."

The road sloped upward, and we passed the *Teatro Vittorio Emanuele*, its facade decorated with intricate stone carvings. Posters outside announced an upcoming opera season, and Grandma made a face like she'd just been assigned homework.

We climbed steadily through narrow side streets lined with corner cafes, tiny fruit shops, and bakeries with trays of fresh pastries in the windows. The smell of warm brioche drifted in through the car vents, almost strong enough to pull us to the curb.

At one intersection, a green-and-white *Interbus* coach lumbered past, headed in the same direction as us. A group of sunhat-wearing tourists pressed their faces to the tinted windows, cameras in hand.

"Glad I'm not on *that* bus" Grandma observed.

She grinned like we had a winning lottery ticket.

The city thinned as we climbed higher, trading storefronts for apartment blocks painted in warm earth tones. Laundry fluttered from balconies, and mopeds zipped between cars like they had a death wish.

At the crest of the hill, Messina opened up behind us—a panorama of the harbor, the ferry docks, and the cobalt blue Strait stretching all the way back to Calabria.

"Not bad," Grandma said, leaning toward the window for a better look.

From there, the road dipped and curved, funneling us toward the highway entrance. Big green *Autostrada A18* signs pointed south, promising Catania and Syracuse in the distance. We merged smoothly, the asphalt wide and clean, the sea glinting occasionally to our left through breaks in the hills. I glanced in the mirror— Grandma was still looking back toward Messina, the faintest smile on her face.

The sun was high, the sky impossibly blue, and everything felt wide open. I was already in love with Sicily—and we hadn't even had lunch yet.

GRANDMA BACKPACKS CINQUE TERRE

RICHARD LUCCHESI

GRANDMA BACKPACKS TUSCANY

RICHARD LUCCHESI

GRANDMA BACKPACKS GERMANY

RICHARD LUCCHESI

GRANDMA BACKPACKS VENICE

RICHARD LUCCHESI

Books by Richard Lucchesi

Under the Tuscan Blunder - One Baby, Two Italian Citizenships, and Three Houses

Grandma Backpacks Italy - Italian Comedy Memoir Short Story

Grandma Backpacks Sicily - Italian Comedy Memoir Short Story

Grandma Backpacks Cinque Terre

Grandma Backpacks Venice

Grandma Backpacks Tuscany

Grandma Backpacks Germany

The Olive Oil Seduction - A Drizzle of Desire, A Dash of Danger

The Balsamic Betrayal - A Tuscan Thriller Where Every Lie is Aged to Perfection

The Truffle Revelation - Secrets Don't Stay Buried

Gunshots and Gelato - One Scoop of Danger, Two Shots of Revenge

The Mozzarella Marriage - The Pasta and Passion Mystery Series Grand Finale

"Love Letters" New Book Series (coming soon.....)

A Note from Richard Lucchesi

Grazie mille for reading *Gunshots and Gelato*!

If Cassidy and Adriano's madness—complete with truffles, tunnels, exploding festivals, questionable life choices, and the occasional near-death snack—made you laugh, gasp, swoon, or crave pasta at wildly irresponsible hours...
I'd be insanely grateful if you left a quick review.

It doesn't need to be long.
It doesn't need to be poetic.
It doesn't even need to be spelled perfectly.

Just a few honest words about what you enjoyed.
Think of it as slipping me a secret note in a crowded piazza—except instead of igniting scandal, you're helping new readers stumble into this ridiculous world of food, danger, romance, and absolute chaos.

For authors like me, reviews aren't just digital confetti—they're lifelines. They're how stories like this find their next reader, how series survive, and how I convince myself that all those late nights, rewrites, and "wait, does this make sense?" moments were worth it.

So from the bottom of my heart:

Thank you for reading.
Thank you for supporting.
And thank you for being part of this delicious, unpredictable adventure.

Until the next twist—
Richard